To my husband, the solid body I can always lean on

Author's note:

I believe authors put a bit of themselves in every story, every character, every scene. In this book I've put more of myself than I ever planned to, or wanted to, but once I started writing, I couldn't help it. I had to be honest.
This is my story, as close to the truth as I dared to write it.

TEN MILE BOTTOM

CHAPTER ONE

The music cut through my insides like a hot knife in butter, melting the edges and seamlessly sinking into me, leaving me open and raw. Every thump of the bass punched me in the gut; every high electronic screech shocked my nerve endings, making my limbs twitch. Nobody noticed my movements were a bit unnatural, or if they did, they didn't care. I danced and shook and shuddered on the crowded dance floor, time slowing down to an agonising crawl. The colourful beams of light passed over sweaty faces slowly, carefully, as if they were flashlights carried by rescuers, lingering on people's features, trying to locate someone in need.

The thing was, everyone was in need here. In need of a release, of a good time, of a quick, uncomplicated fuck in the shadows. Everyone was chasing a high, one way or another. In my case, I wanted to forget; to silence the constant flow of thoughts and images chasing one another in my mind, fighting for dominance every damn second.

You killed him. You fucking killed him.

I was shouting at my mother, my father's casket looming over us from behind the altar. Everyone was staring at us. Renee was holding me back. I couldn't see. My eyes were blind from rage and pain and tears.

I blinked.

To Jay,

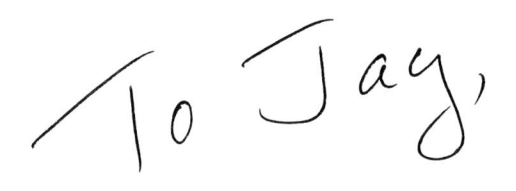

TEN MILE BOTTOM

a novel by

Teodora Kostova

*Thank you for another amazing cover, Jay! I adore you!
Love, Teodora Kostova* :)

Copyright@ Teodora Kostova 2018

ISBN-13: 978-1986581417

ISBN-10: 1986581411

All right reserved. No reproduction, copy or transmission of this publication may be made without written permission of the author. No paragraph of this publication may be reproduced, copied or transmitted without the written permission of the author.

Edited by Kameron Mitchell
Proofread by Charmaine Butler and Vicki Potter
Cover art by Jay Aheer at Simply Defined Art

Disclaimer

This is a work of fiction. All names, places and incidents are either the product of the author's imagination, or are used fictitiously.

It took a fraction of a second but felt like I'd closed my eyes for hours. When my heavy lids finally lifted I saw time had resumed its usual speed. A wall of noise hit me. I staggered backwards. I didn't go too far, half a step at the most, bumping into bodies moving to the fast rhythm. They jostled me back and forth for a while until I found my footing again.

I smiled. Raised my arms over my head and let the music take me again.

It felt good.

It always felt good.

I needed this, today more than ever.

You killed him.

You fucking killed him.

Stop!

"Finn," Someone shouted in my ear, too loud even for the club. "Finn!"

Instinctively, I put my arms around the body currently invading my personal space. I let the familiarity of it, the closeness, the scent, wrap around me like a soft blanket on a cold day, but I still shivered.

"Don't," he said when I placed my lips on the pulse point of his neck. Strong hands gripped my shoulders, but didn't push me away. I straightened and met Aiden's eyes.

Moving images, frozen moments of time – all in vivid colour – burst into my mind the moment I looked at my best friend's face. My dad's smiling, youthful face from my childhood; his coffin being lowered into the ground; my sister crying; my mother crying as I sat there, uncomprehending why she'd cry for someone she spent her entire life hating; Aiden squeezing my hand, looking at me with concern.

You killed him.

I was running, Aiden running behind me, calling my name; his mouth thinning into a colourless line as told him I needed to forget, today more than ever.

I was remembering too much, the effect of the mind numbing drugs wearing off. I needed to stop the wheels turning in my mind. I needed those images gone, if not forever then for a few more hours, or I'd crumple on the floor of the crowded dance floor and die.

"I need another hit," I shouted in Aiden's ear, turning away from him before he could respond.

He wouldn't stop me, I knew that. He'd probably get another hit himself, just like always. He'd be there for me, *with* me, always. But I didn't want to see the light dim in his beautiful eyes again. Wherever I went Aiden followed, even if it meant it'd slowly kill him. I never knew why, but I wasn't too invested in dwelling on it.

I felt his hand gripping my bicep as he followed me through the throng of people to the toilets. The sudden light and silence as we closed the door behind us assaulted my senses, making me twitch.

"Do you have any?" I asked, the adrenalin still buzzing in my blood. Aiden nodded and pulled a small bag out of his pocket. "Good."

We went into one of the cubicles, Aiden leaning back on the closed door. I registered noises coming from some of the other stalls, but I couldn't care less what they were doing. The blood was pounding in my ears, my head throbbing, my hands shaking as I buried them in my hair and pulled. It hurt, and I revelled in the pain.

Aiden's hand, full of pills, appeared in front of my face. I swallowed, already salivating at the thought of blissful abandon. With a wicked grin, I met Aiden's eyes and took two of the pills. He frowned, but was too much out of it to say anything. Before he could summon any common sense and lecture me, I threw the pills in my mouth and swallowed them dry.

I swayed on my feet, the immediate relief and pleasure making me dizzy. The images playing on a loop in my mind dulled, then dispersed around the edges until they were finally gone. God, this was bliss. Real, true, unadulterated bliss.

"Fuck," Aiden swore softly, his head thumping on the door.

I raised my eyes to look at him, caught off guard by how good he looked. Aiden always looked good, with his thick, dark hair, his seductive hazel-brown eyes and the grace with which he moved his tall, lanky body, but in this moment he was the most beautiful man I'd ever seen. I crowded him against the door on wobbly legs, cupping his jaw as I kissed him roughly. Aiden moaned, his hands pulling at the t-shirt on my back.

It felt so good, but so wrong at the same time, and I didn't know why.

"I need booze," I mumbled, nipping at his lower lip as I made to open the door.

Aiden closed his eyes for a brief moment before he nodded and followed me out.

CHAPTER TWO

I never understood the pattern my thoughts tended to form. For instance, why was the bartender's bright green t-shirt the first thing that emerged from the darkness? Was it green at all? Blue? I couldn't really tell.

Everything was so damn dark, no flashing lights, no music. No dancing people, jostling me around as we all moved in different rhythm to the same beat.

I could hear a faint beeping sound but if that was a new hit song someone seriously messed up, because it was boring as fuck. *Beep. Beep. Beep.* That was it. No bass, no other sound. Just darkness and that damn beeping. It was driving me up a wall.

I tried to move, go find Aiden and get the fuck out of this lame club, but for some reason I couldn't. I tried calling his name but my throat was tight and felt strangely raw as if I'd already been shouting for a while. And there was something there... There was something in my mouth, going down my throat.

My eyes flew open, panic overcoming me so suddenly I felt dizzy. I couldn't focus my vision. Everything around me was blurry and too bright. I couldn't move. I couldn't even speak. And that thing in my throat, I didn't know what it was but I wanted it out of me. I felt helpless as I tried to make sense of what was happening, tried to push through the pain and the piercing noise inside my brain.

"Finnegan!"

Someone was saying my name but I couldn't see them. I kept thrashing, trying to get up, trying to focus, disperse the panic, free myself from whatever was holding me down...

"Finnegan, I need you to calm down!" The voice said again, and it sounded strangely like my mother. Only she, and complete strangers, called me by my full name.

Why was she here? And more importantly, why wasn't she trying to help me?

I did as she commanded and stopped moving. Closing my eyes and trying to forget about the thing down my throat, I opened them again, focusing on the nearest object in front of me. It was a plain, square lamp on a plain white ceiling. Turning my head slowly I saw my mother perched on a stool, frowning, and next to her a machine with lots of lights, monitors and cables.

Fucking hell, I was in a hospital. The thing in my mouth was an intubation tube. I couldn't move freely because my hands were tied to the railing of the bed. Everything was slowly starting to make sense as the situation took shape in my mind.

"Finnegan?" My mother said, her voice gentler than before. She placed a hand on the bed railing and leaned closer to me. Her mouth opened, but no words came out. She closed it again and looked away, but not before I saw the disappointment in her eyes.

Nothing new, eh?

My mother's eyes were always filled with either disappointment or impatience or disapproval when she had to deal with me.

I looked away, guiding my vision back to the square lamp on the ceiling. I couldn't deal with her right now, I had more pressing matters at hand. I needed someone to take that tube out of my throat or I was going to lose it again.

I turned to look at my mother and tried to point at the tube the best I could with my restrained hands. She seemed to get what I wanted because she nodded, then stood up and walked out the door, hopefully to get someone in here.

I felt so tired. Achingly, painfully tired. Images, sounds and colours flashed in my mind, unfocused, chasing one another, fighting for my attention. I wanted it all to stop.

I wanted silence.

I wanted darkness again.

Awareness of my body and the pain I was in clawed at the edges of my consciousness again. I wasn't particularly keen on it. It'd felt good to be engulfed in darkness and pain-free weightlessness.

I must have moved, giving away my awareness, because I could hear my mother's voice again, calling my name.

I opened my eyes. It took me a while to be able to focus, the bright daylight hurting my eyes.

"Finnegan?"

Stop saying my name. Stop pretending to care. Go away.

I wanted to scream the words but I didn't have the energy. Besides, even if I did, my throat felt dry and it hurt like a motherfucker.

Tentatively, I tried to swallow past the pain. It hurt. At least the damn tube was gone.

My mother was still standing by the bed, her eyes roaming over my body and my face as if she was searching for something. For what I had no idea, but her frown deepened so I guessed she didn't find it.

"Water," I croaked, barely audible, but she heard me and held a glass of water with a straw to my lips.

I reached for it and surprisingly my hands were free. They weren't of much use though, my hand shaking violently as I tried to hold the glass myself.

"I'll hold it for you," my mother said, making me feel like a fucking invalid.

I drank a couple of sips from the straw, each one cutting through my throat like the dull edge of a knife.

"Thanks," I mumbled, averting my eyes.

"How are you feeling?"

How the fuck do you think I feel?

"Fine."

At least now that the fucking tube was out and I wasn't at risk of another panic attack.

"Finnegan..." My mother sighed, sitting in the white plastic chair by the bed. "You can't go on like this."

I closed my eyes, willing myself to relax and not react to her words. She couldn't wait until I was out of the hospital to lecture me?

"Your sister and I were frantic with worry," she continued, oblivious to my discomfort. "Your behaviour affects more people than yourself, Finnegan." I could hear the tears in her voice but I didn't care. "Why are you so selfish? Your whole life I've tried to do the best for you and you've been defying me every step of the way, only to end up like this." From the corner of my eye I could see her gesturing towards me to emphasise the pathetic state of 'this'.

"Go away," I said with difficulty.

"What?"

"Go. Away." I turned my head to look at her. Her eyes were red, tears streaming down her face. And yet, the disappointed frown she always aimed at me was still firmly in place.

She pursed her lips. "That's what I deserve," she said, straightening her shoulders. "I've always been there for you, and you never appreciate it. For some reason I'm always the bad guy."

A tear rolled down her cheek as she played her well-rehearsed role of the victim.

"I don't want you here," I said, every word feeling like swallowing a blade, but I was determined not to show it. "I don't want your lectures, your false concern..."

"False?" She interrupted me indignantly, her mouth gaping open. "How can you say that, Finnegan? I'm your *mother*."

I felt my hands start to shake as I tried to get a hold of my rising anger. My head started to throb with newfound pain. I reconsidered my conviction that a panic attack was off the table.

"Just fucking go!" I said, with as much force as I could. My voice broke on the last word, and I hated myself for it.

"Mum, that's enough," my sister's calm voice came from the doorway.

Thank. Fucking. God.

I closed my eyes, my body instantly relaxing. Renee could handle our mother from here on out.

"Well, isn't that lovely," Mum said, picking up her bag from the floor. "My own children treating me like this, when I've done nothing – *nothing* – to deserve it." She turned to me, reloading her ammunition as she stood up. "*You* should be apologising to me right now after what you did, and after what you said to me at the funeral." Her voice trembled at the last words, her eyes filling with tears on demand.

As usual when she was double-teamed by her children, my mother hurried out of the room, without letting anyone else say the last word. Once her footsteps were out of earshot, I felt a delirious calm spread over my body and mind like a warm balm, soothing all my senses. My throat didn't seem to hurt that much anymore, my headache was nearly gone and I could even move a little in the bed without piercing pain shooting through my limbs.

Renee sat down with a sigh, in the same chair mother had just vacated. She tried to suppress it but I could hear it loud and clear. I'd heard it too much over the years.

"Go on and say it," I said, trying to turn on my side to see her better. Plus, my back hurt from lying God knew how long in the same position.

"How are you?"

I smiled, then immediately regretted it when my dry upper lip stretched too much for comfort. "That's not what you want to say."

Renee took out a pot of lip balm from her purse and leaned over to spread some on my cracked lips.

"There will be plenty of time to say what I want to say once you're out of here."

The hard note in her voice made my heart hurt. She'd put up with a lot from me, ever since we were kids, but she'd never left my side. And yet, this right now felt different. As if she'd finally had enough.

I couldn't blame her.

I might have said something stupid if the doctor hadn't chosen that moment to come in.

"Mr Hart, glad to see the colour of your eyes." He chuckled at his own joke.

I'd have rolled said eyes if I was sure it wouldn't give me a headache but as the situation stood right now I didn't want to take any chances.

"I'm Doctor Bailey. I performed your surgery and have been keeping an eye on your recovery since then."

He sat down on the other side of my bed, glancing at the monitors and making a few notes on his clipboard, his dark, bushy eyebrows furrowing.

"Surgery?" I mentally examined my body for any missing limbs or unusual pain.

The doctor glanced at Renee. "Yes. We had to remove part of your liver and stop the bleeding from your gastrointestinal tract." He gave me a cheerful smile again and I wanted to smack him.

I turned my confused gaze on Renee. She shrugged and jerked her chin for me to pay attention to the doctor.

"Here's the thing, Mr Hart," the doctor continued, lacing his fingers on top of the clipboard in his lap. His eyes were pale blue, but unlike my mother's they didn't pierce my soul and leave me crushed and empty like a popped balloon. "You're in bad shape. At twenty four, my eighty-year-old grandmother's liver is in better condition than yours." He paused for dramatic effect. I didn't want to chance a glance at Renee so I held the doctor's gaze. "If you don't start looking after yourself, there's a pretty good chance you won't make it to thirty."

There was no cheeky smile, no indication he was exaggerating.

I was at a loss for words. This was too much, all at once. They'd removed part of my liver? My health was so bad I could die soon? What the fuck was I supposed to do with all this?

"Finn," Renee said softly placing a hand on top of mine. I looked at her. Why was she blurry? Did my eyes decide to give up on me, too, just like everyone – everything – else? "We'll get through this," she said, moving her hand to wipe something off my cheek.

Great. Now I was crying like a wimp in front of my baby sister and the bloody doctor.

As if sensing my discomfort, the doctor cleared his throat gently, and said, "I'll come back in a couple of hours for your scheduled examination. We'll talk more then, Mr Hart, and I'll address any concerns you may have." He stood up, glanced at the monitor on my right and made a note on the clipboard. "But I'll advise you to rest, both mentally and physically, until you're out of the ICU. We can discuss everything then." The corner of his mouth lifted into a gentle smile as he placed a hand on my shoulder.

He left, probably to deliver some more bad news to the person lying helpless in the next room. An overwhelming sense of doom settled around me, draining the last of my energy. It felt like my brain was screaming for me to wake up, get up, do something, but my body was simply too exhausted to care. You couldn't force something to work when most of its parts were broken, right?

I felt Renee's hand on top of mine and that was all I needed to give in to the crushing fatigue and blissfully close my eyes.

CHAPTER THREE

My mother came to visit me every day for the next week. She sat next to me, asked me how I felt, talked about her day and the neighbours getting a puppy, and the new range of Asian fusion salads in her favourite restaurant, and the weather. She did not try to accuse me of being a selfish bastard again, but whether it was because Renee had told her off or because she herself felt remorse for attacking her son as he lay helpless in ICU, I couldn't say.

It was in her eyes, though. Every time I looked at her I could see it. The accusation. The disappointment. The regret. I tried avoiding her gaze as much as I could, forced myself to nod politely as she talked, let her pat my hand goodbye every day. And all the time I wished she didn't bother coming.

The thing was, she wasn't doing it because she cared for me all that much. She was doing it because it would look bad if she didn't come. What would the hospital staff think? And her friends? What would she tell the neighbours when they asked after me?

She came out of obligation. If my mother hated something above anything else, it was to go to bed with a guilty conscience.

The soft knock on the door announced Renee's arrival. She walked in, and sat down next to the bed. A few strands of blonde and turquoise streaked hair escaped the loose ponytail she'd probably tied in a hurry, but her blue eyes had a sparkle in them I hadn't seen in a while. Our features were so similar – wide mouth and toothy smile, round face, small nose and pronounced jawline, but while I'd inherited our dad's dark colouring, thick, wavy hair and nearly black eyes, Renee was a carbon copy of our mother with her straight blonde hair, blue eyes, and skin so pale it was almost translucent. And yet as I gazed at her I thought we couldn't have been more different. Renee had always possessed a pure, genuinely good soul I couldn't even dream of, and it showed in her entire demeanour.

"Did you talk to them?" I asked, hopeful. I'd instructed her to use her most disarming smile to get me out of here as soon as humanly possible.

"Yes," she said, turning the disarming smile on me. Too bad I'd seen it all too often and was immune. "Doctor Bailey is coming to examine you later today and if he's happy to sign the discharge papers, you'll be free to go."

"Thank fuck," I mumbled, relaxing deeper into the pillows and closing my eyes, already imagining my upcoming freedom.

I was sick and tired of being treated like an invalid for what seemed like eternity. In fact, it'd been just over a week since I was transferred from the ICU, but I was ready to climb the walls.

"Did you manage to get a hold of Aiden?" I asked.

The long pause made me crack an eye open and look at her.

"Yes," she finally said.

"And?"

She bit her lip and looked away, clearly fighting with the instinct to tell me the truth.

"Renee?"

She sighed. "He'll tell you himself."

"And when would that be?" My annoyance was growing stronger with every second. Aiden, my so called best friend, hadn't come to visit me even once. He hadn't texted or called or sent a raven with a fucking note. We'd been inseparable since meeting in school, and yet he couldn't be bothered to check up on me when I was in the fucking hospital.

"After rehab."

Great.

It wasn't going to be my first time in rehab, so I knew what to expect, and yet I hated the thought of doing it again. Early morning wake up calls, meditation, organic clean food, talking about my feelings... None of these things was appealing to me in any way. But, unfortunately, there was no way around it.

"Speaking of," Renee said, bringing my attention back to her. "Mum and I discussed it and we want you to go to a different rehab this time."

I glared at her, but she ignored me.

"Oh?" I injected as much venom in the single syllable as I could.

"This may be a joke to you, Finn, but it's not to me," Renee said, her steely gaze fixed on me. Her voice didn't waver as she spoke but her eyes shone with tears. "You're treating rehab as a spa holiday, and nothing changes when you come out. I need you to take this seriously."

"I *do* take it seriously!"

"You don't! You heard what the doctor said! I'm not losing my brother because he's too stupid and too stubborn to take care of himself!"

She stood up, her chest heaving, then turned and walked to the window. Silence fell in the room as she stared outside while I fell back onto the pillows and watched her.

What was I supposed to say? Was I supposed to make a promise I surely wouldn't keep? I loved Renee more than I loved anyone and I hated seeing her that upset, but I couldn't promise her I'd never do drugs or drink alcohol ever again. Hell, if they weren't pumping me full of painkillers on a regular basis I'd be craving a hit right now.

TEN MILE BOTTOM

I was a pathetic excuse for a human being and we both knew it. And yet, for some bizarre reason, she still loved me.

When she turned her eyes were red but she wasn't crying. Her hands flapped helplessly at her sides as she tried to find the words she wanted me to hear.

"You overdosed on the filthy floor of a nightclub toilet, your heart stopped on the way to the hospital. You died, Finn," she said, the anguish on her face making me flinch.

"What?"

"You. Died." She repeated, coming closer to the bed. "They said you were in cardiac arrest when the paramedics arrived and they had to resuscitate you. They barely kept you alive on the way to the hospital."

I was too shocked to say anything, and too mentally and physically tired to try to make sense of it. Thankfully she took pity on me and didn't elaborate any further.

"Please, Finn." Her voice was gentle when she spoke again. "Give it a shot. For me."

I couldn't say no.

CHAPTER FOUR

The rehab Renee and mother had chosen for me was more of a medieval monastery than a modern establishment caring for the rich and reckless. Every time I left my room I expected to hear a nun walking behind me, ringing a bell and chanting "shame" until I confessed all my sins. I shared that joke with the psychiatrist, but she didn't get it. Or any of my other Game of Thrones references. I gave up trying to make her smile on the second week. By the end of week three I wasn't sure her facial muscles were capable of forming a smile at all. I'd never seen Doctor Shelton wear any other expression but carefully maintained, highly professional blank mask.

Fuck if I cared. The withdrawals were making me even more high strung than usual. Every other patient in this hellhole gave me a wide berth, mostly because I glared at everyone who made eye contact. It was safe to say the group therapy and meditation sessions didn't go so well, and I was relegated to meditating by myself, with doctor Shelton's personal recommendation.

As if staring at a wall and pretending to empty my mind and focus only on the present moment could curb my desire to feel the fleeting bliss of the numbing drugs dulling my senses and quieting my thoughts.

TEN MILE BOTTOM

At night, I couldn't sleep. I stared at the ceiling until my eyes adjusted to the darkness and I could make out the shapes of the scarce furniture in my room. It was then that the whispers in my head were the loudest, and it was then that the craving for the mind-numbing effect of the drugs and alcohol was the worst. My body shook and spasmed night after night, at first with the physical effects of the withdrawal, and then later, long after the poison had left my body, with helplessness and despair.

Relief didn't come when morning arrived. Only exhaustion and misery.

I hated this. But resisting it would lead to nothing. Doctor Shelton had to sign my discharge papers, and that would only happen when she was satisfied I wouldn't be of any harm to myself and others. That I could go back out there in the big, scary world and not plunge face down into the first black hole of temptation I came across.

Well, tough shit, Doctor. I wasn't kidding myself that I was strong enough to resist the appeal of a clouded mind – a blissfully silent mind – and I didn't really see a point why I should resist it. But I had to convince the doctor otherwise. For now, I had to pretend I cared what happened to me.

For the first four weeks I wasn't allowed any visitors. No TV, mobile phone, internet, newspapers, or any other connection to the outside world. I could get a pre-approved book from the small library and that was the extent of the entertainment I was permitted.

I wasn't in the mood to talk to anyone anyway, or hear about the world's problems. I had nearly convinced myself of that when the first day of the fifth week came and ruined my illusions. As I sat in the common room where people usually congregated to socialise, I held my breath, hoping beyond reason Renee would visit me, and dreading seeing my mother instead, as the door kept opening and closing, welcoming more and more visitors.

Well, Renee didn't come. And neither did my mother. With nearly half the time of the "open day" already gone, I lost hope anyone cared about me and stood to leave the room alive with conversation and laughter. The door cracked open once again and I glanced at it, my heart skipping a beat as I saw Aiden enter the room.

Frozen in place, eyes wide, I watched as he closed the door behind him, his eyes finding me straight away in the crowded room. He started towards me, long, confident strides eating the room in seconds.

He'd changed. Not so much physically, although he'd cut his hair and lost a lot of weight, making his features sharper. It was something within him that had changed the most, but I couldn't name what it was.

People had always said we looked so much alike that we could have been brothers, and I guess that was sort of true. We were both lanky, similar height, with dark hair that stuck every which way without a copious amount of product, and we both had a round face that made us look much younger than we actually were. For me, the biggest difference was our eyes. Not just the colour – mine a hard black, and Aiden's a warm hazel-brown – but what lurked behind them. I always saw a kindness in Aiden's gaze that I never managed to find in mine.

Aiden crossed the room and enveloped me in his arms without hesitation. He hugged me so fiercely that I felt something inside me break.

"Finney," he said, exhaling my name with relief.

"You cut your hair," was all I managed to say.

Aiden chuckled, then let me go. His eyes searched mine and I was suddenly aware of how bad I must look. Looking away self-consciously, I inclined my head towards the French windows on the left.

"Wanna take a walk?"

Aiden nodded and followed me. A few people had also chosen to spend the day outside, enjoying the late April sunshine. The soft breeze felt pleasant on my skin, and in my hair which I'd let grow unrestrained in the past few months, and completely forgone the use of any products. I rarely looked in the mirror nowadays either.

I felt Aiden's presence next to me, my mind conjuring an image of him, his hair so much like mine, moving with the breeze, his hand coming to flatten it and slick it back almost unconsciously. But as I turned, the mental image of my friend disappeared, to be replaced with his new buzz cut, his features stark and sharp without the soft, dark waves framing his face. I felt nostalgic, and a bit sad.

"You've lost weight," he said, glancing at me.

I snorted. "So have you."

He laughed sardonically, nodding slightly, agreeing without hesitation that we were both messed up losers.

"Let's sit," he said, grabbing my hand and pulling me towards an empty bench nearby.

I didn't protest, even though I wasn't really keen on looking at him as we talked. Aiden's warm eyes used to be the only reason I pulled back from the edge so many times; I used to crave the way he focused on me so absolutely that he shut the rest of the world out. That seemed like a lifetime ago. Now, the thought of Aiden's piercing gaze focused on me filled me with dread.

We sat. Aiden angled his body towards me, as I'd expected. I folded my arms over my chest and kept staring ahead as if the green lawn in front of us was the most interesting thing I'd ever seen.

"How are you?" Aiden asked, tentatively, as if he didn't know everything about me. He'd always been able to tell how I was feeling with a single look in my direction.

"Where have you been?" I asked instead of answering, annoyance creeping around the edges of my words.

From the corner of my eye I saw Aiden nodding, as if knowing I was going to say that. Yeah, well, small talk was never my forte.

"I had a heart attack," he said, matter of fact.

I whipped my head to look at him so fast something in my neck cracked painfully. I ignored it.

"You what?" I said, my mouth gaping open. He smiled fondly before repeating his words.

"I had a heart..."

"I fucking heard you!"

He nodded again, licked his lips and looked away. Aiden rarely got angry or lost control of his emotions, so I was used to him reacting calmly to my regular outbursts. At that moment, though, his relaxed body language and even voice made me see red.

"Are you fucking serious?" I yelled. Aiden glanced around as if to see if there were any people nearby, but I couldn't care less if the whole world heard me. "You disappear for nearly two months, no phone calls or texts or even a note under my pillow, and then you waltz in here, thin and pale and with a fucking buzz cut, and tell me you had a heart attack without any preamble? What the fuck, Aiden?"

"How was I supposed to lead up to it, then?" He said, a rare edge of irritation lacing his words.

Usually, I had a witty, sarcastic remark at the ready for any occasion. Not this time. I opened, then closed my mouth a few times, unable to come up with a suitable introduction to 'I had a heart attack'. Aiden let me gape like a fish for a while, patiently waiting for me to either shout it all out of my system, or calm down enough for him to speak. Folding my arms again, I leaned back on the bench, pouted for good measure, and waited for him to start talking.

Aiden chewed on his lip for a few moments as if collecting his thoughts, or maybe choosing the right words not to upset me again, before he spoke.

"The night you OD-ed? Do you remember anything?"

"Not really, not after we took a hit in the bathroom that second time." I racked my brain for some more clues as to what had happened that night, but I'd done that a million times after waking up at the hospital with no success. "I think we went to that bar and had some shots afterwards?"

"Yeah," he nodded, then looked at me with a sad smile. "We had a lot of shots. We danced. Then you wanted another hit and I couldn't stop you. We fought and you stalked away to the toilets with some guy. I was pretty messed up myself so I let you go." A muscle jumped in Aiden's jaw, and I was pretty sure the emotion lurking underneath his words was guilt. Before I could say anything he continued. "I don't know how much time passed before I went looking for you. I was high out of my mind, stumbling my way through the club, but I remember as clear as day the moment I saw you lying on the floor. I dropped on my knees next to you, screaming for help. I didn't know what to do, I've no fucking idea how to give CPR or even check for a pulse. Thankfully someone walked in shortly after me and they must have called an ambulance because one moment I was cradling your head in my lap, my whole body shaking with fear that you were dead, and the next there were paramedics storming in, pushing me out of the way and loading you onto a stretcher."

Aiden took a deep breath, exhaling loudly. He seemed to need a moment to compose himself, and so did I. Up until now I hadn't known exactly how it'd all gone down that night, and I still didn't remember anything, but the way he talked about it, the anguish in his eyes...

"So," Aiden cleared his throat, glancing at me, the pain in his gaze making me flinch. "I'm not exactly sure what happened after they took you away. I remember feeling really out of it, but in a weird way, not just because of the drugs. I also remember a lot of pain, and a strange sort of out of body experience when I couldn't really control my limbs and crumbled to the floor."

I was thankful for the pause Aiden made. I wanted to put a hand over his mouth and stop him talking all together, but how could I? I'd done this to him. *Me.* The very least I could do was hear what else he had to say.

But... I didn't know if I could. I felt like I'd hit rock bottom and nothing could push me back to the surface ever again.

"Finney," he said, placing his hand on my arm. I turned to face him. His face softened when he met my eyes and almost resembled the round, baby face I was so used to looking at. Almost. He'd lost so much weight that his features would probably never be as soft and innocent as they were before. "What happened to me is not your fault."

I snorted. I'd never heard such a huge lie in so few words.

"I'm twenty four, an adult, I've made my own choices," he continued, his fingers digging into my arm. "And so have you." I looked away. "Obviously, we can't change the past, but we can definitely do something for the future."

Oh for fuck's sake, save me the pep talk.

My eyeroll must have relayed my thoughts exactly because Aiden removed his hand and his expression hardened.

"You cannot continue like this, Finn," he said.

I stubbornly didn't say anything, only arched an eyebrow. The more people told me I couldn't live my life the way I wanted to, the more self-destructive I became.

Aiden saw this. He always saw everything, dammit. But at that moment I saw something change in his eyes, some secret he'd been hiding, unsure whether to tell me bubbling to the surface. He had an ace up his sleeve and he was about to throw it on the table.

"*I* cannot continue like this. I need some time away from..." He gestured between us, around us, I didn't fucking know, but I knew what he meant.

"You mean from me." I was ready to see him gone. I *wanted* him gone. I wanted to see his retreating back, his stupid buzz cut and patronising gaze gone from my life. I made to stand up, but he caught my arm firmly and pulled me back.

"Yes. From you. And from all of our other 'friends'."

I couldn't believe he actually said it. My gentle, kind Aiden, the only person who'd always been there for me, *with* me, was leaving me.

"And you need to do the same."

I laughed. I couldn't help it. A burst of disappointed, incredulous laughter tore out of me, but as I laughed, I felt my heart squeezing painfully.

"Do what you think is best for you, mate, but don't tell me how to live my life."

And there it was. The hard look in his eyes, the clenching of his jaw. The moment he got ready to destroy me.

"Renee had a miscarriage when you OD-ed," he said, no regret in his eyes, only determination.

I recoiled from him as if he'd actually struck me. My ears were ringing and for the first time in my life my mind was completely blank without the help of any illegal substance.

"She'll hate me for telling you. She swore me to secrecy, but I think you need to know." Aiden continued as if he hadn't just shattered my whole world to pieces. "We love you, Finney, but we need you to start taking care of yourself, at the very least. Renee is your baby sister and yet she's been looking after you her whole life. She'd be devastated if anything happened to you."

I heard the words but I couldn't react. My mind was blissfully blank for a while, and then it was flooded with accusation, guilt, memories of Renee and I as kids, as teenagers, as adults. And then my traitorous thoughts drifted towards the future in which I saw Renee as a mum, playing with a little girl, both their smiles so bright and happy.

Until I ruined it all. My best friend had a heart attack at twenty four because I'd been dragging him down with me, then scared the shit out of him; my sister lost her unborn child because I nearly died and made her frantic with worry.

I'd never felt more like a useless, spineless piece of shit.

"You've only ever wanted the big things," Aiden said, taking my hand in his and looking at me with so much tenderness I felt my eyes fill with tears. "You always thought there's no point writing a book unless it hit every bestseller list around the world. No point wasting four years at uni unless you graduated with honours. You always aim for the highest possible point, and put too much pressure on yourself to make sure you reach it." Aiden paused to lick his lips and pat my hand in his. "But the thing is, once you get there, there's nowhere higher for you to go, and all you can do is crash back down."

I met Aiden's eyes, tried to find my voice and say something, but I couldn't. I'd reached the end of my rope, beyond words, beyond anger, beyond guilt. I was empty and broken and lost, and I needed something, *anything*, to anchor me to the present before I drifted off without a lifeline.

I started crying.

It was one of those violent, ugly bursts of unsuppressed sobs that rattled my insides and made my soul hurt. I was distantly aware that Aiden held me, but I wasn't sure. I was in so much pain that everything simply stopped existing.

CHAPTER FIVE

It was a beautiful June morning and I hated every second of it.

Much like the night before, I couldn't sleep, so at 5 AM I gave up trying and got up. My new landlord had described the house as 'needing some love and care', but the truth was it was a bloody nightmare. Aiden'd managed to convince me that I needed a project, some laborious work to get my mind off things and help me detox my thoughts, and voilà, a month later I'd rented a house at the very edge of Ten Mile Bottom – a picturesque little town in Cambridgeshire. I'd even gotten a discount on the rent for agreeing to do all the work myself.

I wasn't sure who I hated more – Aiden, the landlord, or myself.

Probably Aiden. I'd agreed to uproot my entire life in London, and the bastard had let me pick the town by randomly pointing to it on a map, and, at the time, finding the name hilarious.

I sighed heavily as I surveyed the living room. The night before I'd managed to cover the hardwood floors – probably the only decent feature in this house – with a thick dustsheet in preparation for painting the walls today. The thing is, I wasn't built for hands-on work. I couldn't even figure out how to work the oven in my London flat. I'd never held a paintbrush in my entire life, and I didn't even want to think about trying to fix anything with a hammer or a screwdriver, and I was a bio hazard with a bleach bottle in hand.

I was really tempted to call someone in to do all the work while I lounged in the garden reading a book, but I knew Aiden was right. If I did that my mind would just spiral out of control again, making my anxiety soar. I needed to do the work myself and maybe I wouldn't feel like a useless piece of shit for a while.

With renewed enthusiasm, I walked to the kitchen and got my tablet from the table. YouTube must have a few wall painting tutorials, right? It couldn't be *that* hard to spread some paint on a flat surface.

It turned out it was very fucking hard. There were all these things to consider, like making the first coat as even as possible; cutting off the edges to the ceiling and the skirting boards with military precision; pacing yourself and the amount of paint you used so that you wouldn't run out in the middle of your project.

I failed miserably on the last one. I ran out of paint half way through the second coat. A lot of it was on the floor because it was damn hard to lift the roller from the tray without dripping paint everywhere, even if the guy on YouTube made it look so easy and clean. I was getting hungry anyway so I decided to give myself a little break, go find something for lunch and stop by a DIY store to get more paint.

A much needed shower and a change of clothes later, I climbed into my car feeling quite accomplished. Which was when my fucking car decided to show me the finger.

I loved that car. I really, truly did. I harboured an irrational attachment to it without any sentimental reason. The BMW M6 had been the first thing I'd bought with the advance for my first novel. That'd been five years ago and I still loved the car as much as the first time I'd laid eyes on her in the shiny dealership. Despite being very temperamental, leaving me stranded on the road multiple times and spending a hideous amount of money for repairs, the thought of getting another car never even crossed my mind.

Until this very moment. The engine automatically turned off, and the bright red light in the shape of a wheel currently blinking on the dashboard felt like the last drop of misfortune in my miserable existence.

"Fuck!" I yelled, hitting the wheel and accidentally sounding the horn. "I hate you, you stupid piece of shit car!" The blazing sound of the horn manifested the anger inside me in such a perfect way that I pressed on it, over and over again, shouting obscenities at my car, until I was physically and mentally exhausted.

Dropping my head on the wheel I took a deep breath, trying to calm down. A soft knock on the window right next to me startled me, and I jumped, my heart beating frantically as I faced the intruder of my personal melt down.

A man, probably in his late sixties, was staring at me, his finger bent as if poised to knock again. His wrinkled face was etched with concern and maybe a bit of caution, but his eyes were kind as they looked me up and down through the glass.

"Yes?" I said, lowering the window, feeling my irritation bubbling inside me, but managing to curtail the urge to snarl in the old man's face.

"You alright, mate?" The man asked, unfazed by my hostile demeanour. His gaze swept around inside the car as if looking for clues for my insanity.

"I'm fine, thanks," I said, making to close the window, but thinking better of it.

"You sure? There's a red light blinking on your dashboard," the man said, pointing at the light as if I hadn't fucking seen it. I ground my teeth together. "And you sounded your horn as if you needed help."

I glared at him, but he only smiled at me, the kindness in his eyes making my annoyance surge even further.

"Look," he said before I had a chance reply. "Why don't you come over for a cup of tea and wait for the tow truck inside? You know how they are, it may take them an hour to get here and get you sorted."

"A tow truck?" I asked, as if I'd never heard the word before. I didn't realise the issue was so serious.

"Well, yes," the man said, confused. "Your power steering's given out. You can't go anywhere. And looking at the car I'm quite sure they won't be able to fix it by the road. It's all electronic, isn't it?"

"It's all what electronic?" I was aware I sounded like an idiot, but the man was giving me too much information all at once. Power steering failure? Tow truck? Invitation for tea in his house? What if I was a murderous criminal preying on the elderly and all of this was only an act?

"The power steering system in your car," the man said, his words slower and clearer than before.

"I've no idea," I said honestly, leaning back in the seat. This was a fucking nightmare.

"Alright, then," the man said, tapping on the door with his palm. "Let's get you a hot cup of tea and call for assistance. We'll get you sorted in no time." He smiled at me and I had a fleeting thought that *he* might be the murderous criminal preying on the young and vulnerable, and once I set foot into his house they'd never find my body.

At this point I didn't even care. I got out of the car, locked it unnecessarily, and followed the man into his house across the road from mine.

TEN MILE BOTTOM

"You moved in last week, eh?" Mr Grayson – or Steve as he insisted I call him – asked as he put a steaming cup of tea in front of me. I nodded, wrapping my fingers around the hot mug, even though it was a hundred degrees outside. "What brings you to Ten Mile Bottom?"

He eyed me curiously over the rim of his mug as he took a careful sip.

I shrugged. "I needed a change of scenery."

I shifted on the chair. His searching gaze was making me uncomfortable and I dreaded he may ask more questions. I wasn't used to this whole friendly neighbour routine. I'd lived in my London flat for five years and I didn't know any of my neighbours' names, let alone exchanged life stories over hot beverages. Hell, I considered it an achievement if I recognised any of them on the street.

As if sensing my discomfort, Steve nodded, more to himself than me, and asked, "Do you like pie?"

The sudden change in the direction of the conversation made me dizzy. "Sure," I said.

"Good." He stood up and walked to the counter at the other side of the kitchen, his back to me. "My Ruby loves baking. She makes something every day, bless her," he said as he started taking plates out of cupboards. "She's at her book club right now – baked a peach tart for them yesterday – and she'd hate she missed you. She wanted to come over and introduce herself the day you moved in, but I managed to stop her. 'Give the kid a day or two to adjust, love', I told her. I know city folk can get a bit skittish if you corner them."

I could hear the smile in his voice even if I couldn't see his face. I couldn't help but smile, too. "How did you know I was 'city folk'?" I asked, doing the air quotes as he turned to face me holding two plates.

Raising a bushy grey eyebrow at me, Steve didn't reply. He brought the plates to the table, and then went back to the fridge.

"Custard?"

"Yes, please," I said, thinking that maybe waiting for the tow truck with a hot mug of tea and a slice of cherry pie smothered in custard wasn't such a bad thing after all.

CHAPTER SIX

Roadside assistance turned up in about an hour, just like Steve had predicted. The guy looked under the hood as Steve and I watched, and declared he couldn't do anything out here and the car needed to go to a garage.

"I miss how they used to make them," he said, slamming down the hood, making me wince. "You could fix nearly any issue by tying a wire to whatever was broken. Now you need computers and apps and whatnot."

I barely managed to keep myself from rolling my eyes. Barely.

"So..." I drawled, waving a hand between us and the car. The guy looked at me blankly. "Is there a garage nearby?"

"Take it to Bob," Steve said to the guy. He looked at me, then at the car, and then nodded.

"Seems like the best option."

Whoever that Bob guy was I wanted to get there as soon as possible and get my car fixed. After wasting so much time waiting for the tow truck, I needed people to show some initiative and stop acting like time had slowed down in Ten Mile Bottom. Unsurprisingly, Steve knew the tow truck guy – Howard? Harrison? – and while I was getting more and more frustrated, they kept chatting by the side of the road as if we were at a family barbeque.

I cleared my throat. Both of them looked at me as if I was an attention seeking child.

"Would you mind if we get going?" I asked gesturing at the car.

With a reluctant sigh, Howard/Harrison bid Steve goodbye and loaded my car onto his truck bed. Looking at her, unable to move on her own, being tied to a rope and dragged, helpless, onto the truck I might have cried. Instead, trying to push the feeling away, I turned to Steve.

"Thanks for the pie and everything."

"You'll have to come by again," he said, a slow smile making his eyes sparkle. "Ruby will want to meet you, too."

I grimaced, making Steve's smile spread into a full blown grin. The bastard knew he was making me uncomfortable and he didn't care.

"Sure," I said, in what I hoped was a noncommittal tone.

The ride to Bob's garage was uncomfortable in more ways than one. Howard/Harrison made me sit at the front of his truck which probably hadn't been cleaned since he'd bought it, and I spent the fifteen minute ride avoiding all the questions he threw my way. I'd never been happier than when I saw the big blue sign 'Robert Goodwin & Sons' not a hundred yards away. I couldn't get out of the truck fast enough, leaving Howard/Harrison to unload my car, and headed for the reception.

A guy around my parents' age sat behind a desk, clicking with a mouse and staring at a huge monitor. He was wearing thick framed glasses that made his green eyes look huge.

"Alright?" He said as I approached him.

"Been better."

Bob – I assumed – smiled at me, removed his glasses and jerked his chin at my car currently being unloaded in front of his office.

"Yours?"

I nodded.

"What happened?"

I explained what the problem seemed to be while Bob offered me a seat and tea. I sat, but declined the tea. When I was done he reached for the walkie talkie on his right and asked someone called Ben to come in here.

"My son will look at your car in a minute," he said, subtly sizing me up. I could see the curiosity in his eyes, but even though my car's fate lay in that man's hands, I frowned at him, hoping to curtail his urge to pry into my life. I'd had this done to me too many times today, and keeping my private shit private was getting exhausting.

Luckily, two men walked into the office from a side door leading to the garage. They were laughing, and the taller one playfully pushed the other one as he stepped through the threshold.

"Cut it out, dickhead!" He said, barely managing to keep upright after the shove.

"Boys!" Bob said in a warning tone.

The guy who nearly fell met his dad's eyes, then turned to look at me, and froze. Huge green eyes stared at me as if he'd seen a ghost. The other guy bumped into him, surprised by his sudden immobility in the middle of the room.

"The fuck's wrong with you, Ben?"

Bob rolled his eyes, sighed, then called Ben over, explaining my car's problem as he approached the desk. Ben nodded, and when he turned to face me again he wouldn't meet my eyes.

"Why don't you leave her here tonight, and we'll call you tomorrow after we test her?" His skin was darker than his dad's, but I could still see the blush that crept up his cheekbones. I frowned, opening my mouth to protest and demand my car be seen today, but something in Ben's body language gave me a pause. "It's just that we have other cars to finish before the end of the day, and I'm not sure how long that'll take." This time when he spoke he raised his green eyes, the only feature he'd inherited from his dad it seemed, and met mine. I had no idea why the guy was getting so flustered, and neither did his dad and his brother if the confused looks they exchanged were any indication.

I was getting a bit annoyed – I felt like a latecomer, walking in to hear the end of the joke and see everyone laughing, and having no idea what was so funny. What was worse, I felt analysed, dissected, talked about behind my back the moment I turned to leave. A wave of homesickness hit me so hard and so unexpectedly that I had to grab the edge of the desk to anchor myself.

Embarrassed, I looked at Ben, holding his gaze as I frowned. A snappy remark was on the tip of my tongue, and I was ready to deliver it with impeccable arrogance, but the vulnerability in his beautiful eyes stopped my words in their tracks. How could he be so open with a stranger? My frown deepened, but the angry words I was about to say to him died inside me unspoken.

"That's alright," I finally managed to say, looking away. "I have no way of getting back to the house, though." I paused, realising I had errands to run before I got back, and the uncomfortable feeling in my stomach reminded me I hadn't had decent lunch, the pie I ate with Steve long forgotten. "Can you give me the number for a cab service?" I took out my phone, ready to dial a cab and get the hell out of here.

"Yes, of course," Bob said, but got interrupted by the road assistance guy who walked in to get me to sign the paperwork for the job.

From the corner of my eye I saw Ben's brother grabbing his arm and pulling him back through the door that led to the garage. Through the glass door I saw them arguing about something, Ben's brother waving his arms around while Ben stood, his arms crossed, staring at the floor. I shook my head, confused. I had no fucking idea what was going on and frankly I was fed up with this whole thing. I bid Bob a hasty goodbye and walked out without giving him a chance to protest. I'd find my own damn cab.

Outside, I fished my phone out of my pocket only to see a black screen. I pressed and held the power button until the phone vibrated in my hand, lit up, only to shut down a second later, flashing an empty battery icon.

"Fucking idiot," I murmured to myself, clutching the phone to stop myself from throwing it against the concrete. It was my fault, I knew that, I was the one who forgot to charge his phone last night, and yet I felt as if the whole universe was conspiring against me. *Kept* conspiring against me.

Embarrassingly, I felt close to tears. But I'd be damned if I walked back in there and asked for help after the dramatic storm off I'd just performed. I'd walk back to the house if I had to.

The town centre couldn't be too far, right? I'd walk down there and find a power bank to charge my phone and call a taxi. Hell, I'd buy a new fucking phone before I walked back to ask Bob for help.

I started walking.

In a couple of minutes I realised it was a bad idea. There was no pavement along the road; I was basically risking my life walking along the road, hoping some crazy bastard wouldn't take a turn a bit too swiftly and turn me into roadkill.

Still, I was committed to my stubborn ways. Until a car pulled slowly alongside me. I turned and scowled at the driver who was lowering the window.

"You can't afford me, darling, move along," I said, waving my hand dismissively.

The driver laughed, and I swear to god it was the loveliest, purest, fucking sexiest sound I'd ever heard, stopping me in my tracks. I bent down to take a look at the creature who made my dick hard in two seconds flat, thinking I might have overreacted and he could indeed afford me if he laughed like that again.

My eyes met clear green ones and my scowl returned.

"Why are you following me instead of working on my car?"

Ben smiled, his eyes twinkling with what could only be described as mischief. "Why are you walking?"

"Long story," I said, straightened, and kept on walking. He kept on following me. A car came behind him, blasting its horn as it sped around us.

"Get in," he said.

I ignored him, fully aware I was being stubborn *and* the parallels with Legally Blonde.

"Mr Hart, get in the car before some asshole in a forty-ton lorry hits you without even realising."

Mr Hart. Great. Fucking great.

I stopped abruptly, reached for the door handle. Ben jumped on the brakes as I pulled it open and climbed inside.

"Please don't call me that," I said, buckling my seat belt. "Finn is fine."

Ben nodded, accelerating slowly. The radio was playing some R&B song I didn't recognise, the air conditioner blasted cold air in my face, making me uncomfortable. I reached for the vent, tilting it up and away from my face.

"Where to?" Ben asked, his hand moving on the gear shift. Fuck, but I found that little gesture sexy. His long fingers gently gripped the black stick, moving it so smoothly it made my stomach clench.

"Just leave me somewhere close to the town centre, whatever's on your way."

Ben nodded again and we rode in silence for a while. I'd been right – the town centre was less than a five minute drive so it wouldn't have taken me more than half an hour walking. A strange sort of satisfaction bloomed inside me. I wasn't a complete idiot after all.

"I'd advise against walking down that road ever again," Ben said as if reading my mind. "There have been nearly a dozen fatal incidents in the last six months alone, most of them involving people walking their dogs or cyclists." He paused to glance at me for a moment before aiming his full attention back on the road. A muscle jumped in his jaw and I couldn't tear my eyes off of that spot. "I've been chasing the council to put a speed camera on that stretch for ages."

I sighed. "Desperate times..." I said, waving my hand around instead of continuing my thought.

Ben pulled into a parking spot right in front of a department store without a comment.

"Thank you," I said, unbuckling my seat belt. "You didn't have to go out of your way to drop me off here." For some reason I felt increasingly embarrassed and didn't make any eye contact. I felt my anxiety spike and I wanted nothing more but to get out of this car.

With my hand on the door handle I chanced a glance at Ben. He was watching me intently, a little crease between his brows, as if trying his hardest to figure me out but failing.

"Alright, thanks again," I said, opening the door and stepping outside. "Please call me as soon as you figure out what's wrong with my car, will you?" I saw him nod before I slammed the door a bit too hard.

My legs were shaking as I made my way inside the department store, not looking back, but being distinctly aware of Ben's car driving off.

Low blood sugar, I thought, remembering I hadn't eaten since breakfast and that had only been some yoghurt and a banana.

Right. Food first, feeling sorry for myself later.

CHAPTER SEVEN

By the time the sun started to set that evening, I was completely and utterly exhausted. This day felt like it'd been dragging for a week. On the plus side, all the walls in the living room, dining room, and kitchen were freshly painted, and I could finally sit down and relax with a cold drink. A cold, non-alcoholic drink.

I took a bottle of Coke from the fridge and took it outside in the garden, sitting down and unscrewing the cap with a satisfying hiss. After taking a few big gulps, my stomach growled audibly. I sighed, letting my head roll on the chair's back. The sun had nearly set behind the line of trees in the distance, casting an orange glow over the sky. It was mesmerising to watch the last rays disappear. I couldn't remember when was the last time I'd watched a sunset, if ever. When was the last time I'd sat outside after a horrible day and allowed myself to just be?

Sometimes the small things are the really important things, Finney.

Aiden's words rang true in my head as I watched the gorgeous colours spread over the sky, painting the fluffy white clouds shades of orange, yellow, red, and even pink.

My stomach growled again, reminding me that as much as I wanted to sit here and not move for the next five years, I was getting hungrier by the second and the fridge was as empty as I'd left it this afternoon. All I'd managed to do after Ben had dropped me off earlier was get a quick lunch, buy a power bank, grab a couple of buckets of paint from the DIY store, and call a cab back home.

I took the newly charged phone out of my pocket and googled food delivery services in the area. A few places popped up, and I quickly ordered way too much Chinese food, but I was too exhausted to care. That sorted, I leaned back in the chair and watched the darkening sky, content to not think about anything beyond the upcoming Chinese food feast.

Not more than five minutes later the distant sound of the doorbell startled me. Standing up, I checked the time on my phone to make sure I hadn't dozed off for half an hour, but no, it'd been exactly six minutes since I'd ordered the food. Frowning, I walked to the door, ready to send whoever it was away without any pleasantries.

"Hi," Ben said with a smile as I hastily pulled the door open.

"Hi?" His genuine smile and open expression took me by surprise yet again.

"Sorry for bothering you this late but I thought you might want her back as soon as possible," he said, extending his hand, my car keys hanging from one long finger. I'd been so caught in Ben's presence that I'd completely missed my car sitting right there behind him in my driveway.

"You managed to fix her?" I asked, taking the keys and stepping past him to walk over to the car.

"There was nothing to fix, actually," he said, walking right behind me. I looked at him with surprise and he continued. "I connected the car to the computer and no fault came on. So I started it and took it for a test drive and everything worked fine. My guess is, a pebble or something hit one of the sensors and lodged itself there, disturbing the system. But when the car was towed to the garage the pebble probably fell off." He shrugged. I frowned. "I know it sounds ridiculous but I've seen it happen before. This car is not made for uneven, dirty country roads, Finn."

With inhuman strength I managed to curtail the urge to close my eyes at the sound of his voice saying my name. I took a careful step away from him, turning to the car, tracing my fingers along the roof.

"But I love her," I said, sounding like a petulant child. I didn't want to sell the one thing that remained of my old life. The one thing that made me feel a little luxury, a little like myself when I was driving her.

Ben grinned. "Of course you do. I'm not suggesting you should get rid of her, but we may have to see each other often, I'm afraid." My eyes snapped to his. *Such hardship, how would I ever endure it,* I thought.

He jerked his chin toward the car. "She's not used to the country life yet."

I bit my cheek against a smile and said, "How much do I owe you?"

Ben waved a hand. "I didn't do anything. The car was fine. I only took it for a test drive and I can assure you that wasn't unpleasant."

"You also wasted your time trying to diagnose the problem and then drove her back to me after work." I didn't want to owe anyone any favours. I still hadn't figured out how to return the favour to Steve for taking me in this afternoon, and it was making me increasingly uncomfortable.

"It's not a problem," Ben said, waving his hand dismissively again.

A car pulled up in front of the driveway and a short middle-aged guy came out, waved at us, then took two take-away bags out of the boot. He gave one to me and one to Ben with a smile, the delicious scent of steaming hot food overwhelming all my senses. I inhaled and closed my eyes for a moment, my stomach growling again. I managed to tip him before he walked away with another wave.

"Expecting company?" Ben asked with a raised eyebrow, looking between the extortionate amount of food and me.

"No, but I feel like I can eat an elephant and my attention span is fucked so I couldn't be bothered choosing, and ordered the entire menu."

Ben handed me the bag and I just stood there, between him and my car, the food smell filling the air between us and my knees weakening with hunger.

"Why don't you at least stay for dinner?" I heard myself saying, but my brain was too slow to catch up. Ben's eyes lit up, the green shining like a cat's in the dusk. "It's the least I can do after all the trouble you went through for my car," I added hastily. My heart was beating so fast I thought I'd keel over and die.

"Sure, I'd love to," Ben said, grabbing the bag from my hand and starting towards the house as if sensing I might change my mind.

"Awesome," I murmured, trailing behind him.

The thing was, sometimes we make stupid, hasty decisions and they break us; nearly kill us. But sometimes, we make stupid, hasty decisions that turn out to be the best thing that'd happened to us in a while.

As I sat in the uncomfortable wooden chair, mentally cataloguing the need for new dining room chairs that didn't make my ass feel numb and my back bend in a weird angle, I watched Ben as he talked animatedly, the smile never leaving his face.

"It's handy to know a few languages, you know?" He said, finishing his story about a car full of tourists, stranded on the motorway in the middle of the night and who could only speak a few words in English. "Especially when you live in a place like this." He paused to take a bite of his prawn toast, holding it gently between his fingers.

With effort I managed to disentangle my attention from his luscious lips as he chewed his food and focus on his words.

"A place like what?" I asked with a raised eyebrow. He was aware we were currently sitting in a dining room in a house in the outskirts of a small, rural town with population of thirty thousand, right?

"Cambridge is a few miles away and it's severely overcrowded, so people tend to migrate to the neighbouring towns," Ben said with a shrug, and took another bite of prawn toast. "And Cambridge, I don't know if you've been, but there are people there from all over the world. Lots of them come and go because of the university, but a lot of them stay. Like my mum."

"Your mum?"

"Yeah, she's Colombian," Ben said with a grin. "Hence the Spanish." He waved a hand indicating the link to the story he'd told me.

And the gorgeous dark skin, I added in my head, before clearing my throat and saying aloud, "Yeah?"

I wasn't going to win any eloquence awards tonight and I was okay with that. Ben didn't seem to mind either.

Ben smiled widely as he spoke of his mother. "Yeah. She came to Cambridge to study medicine – her family is loaded," he said with another dismissive wave. "Met my dad, fell in love, and stayed after graduation. He always teases her that she's a Colombian mafia princess."

"Is she?" I asked, mimicking his smile.

"Nah, her dad is a doctor and her mum came from money, so they're doing well, without any mafia connections." He looked away thoughtfully then added, "As far as I know."

He met my eyes and the teasing glint in them told me he was kidding. I laughed and shook my head, scooping some rice onto my fork. We ate in silence for a while, and I knew I was probably expected to return the favour and offer some personal information but the thought of sharing any of my fucked up history or family drama with this sweet, caring man made my stomach clench uncomfortably.

"Finn?" Ben said, making me look at him. He'd put his fork down and propped his chin on his hands. "I kinda need to come clean about something, and I realise I should have probably said it back in the garage when we first met, but it didn't seem like the right time, and now I'm afraid you may think I'm some weirdo or a stalker or something." He was rambling, his body tense, not a trace of the smiling, relaxed posture from a minute ago. It was making me nervous.

Maybe stupid, hasty decisions end up killing us after all.

"Oh, god, you're already looking at me as if I'm a stalker." His eyes got impossibly bigger, and all of a sudden I felt a pang of protectiveness in my chest.

"I don't think you're a stalker, Ben," I said, leaning back in my chair and folding my arms. "Just say whatever you have to say."

He took a deep breath then puffed it out. "I know who you are." I was pretty certain he wasn't breathing as he was looking at me with big, round eyes full of regret. "I'm sorry, but I do," he continued in a rush, raising his hands as if to ward off the frown forming on my face. "And I'm a huge fan. 'Lost Silence' changed my life, Finn. I can't ever tell you how much that book means to me."

"Fuck," I groaned as I covered my face with my hands.

Just my luck. Moving to Ten Mile Bottom, literally randomly pointing it on a map, and someone here knew what an author who hadn't published anything in two years looked like.

"I've been following you on social media for years so I knew it was you the moment I saw you, but then you looked so haggard and pissed off, and I couldn't say anything." He kept talking and I peeked at him through the fingers still covering my face.

I didn't want to be Finnegan J. Rowe right now. I wanted to go back to five minutes ago when we were eating Chinese food and swapping funny stories. Well, Ben telling funny stories and me grunting a single syllable reply as I stuffed my face, but whatever.

"Will you say anything?" He said, a worried crease deepening between his brows. Reaching over the table he gently tugged my hand away from my face.

"I don't think you're a weirdo," I said, truthfully. I'd met plenty of my readers and Ben's reaction was severely subdued compared to some others'. Don't get me started on some of the gifts I'd received. I shuddered thinking about it.

"But?" Ben prompted.

"But I'd rather you didn't tell anyone else about this."

"Josh already knows," Ben said as he looked away guiltily. "But I didn't tell him! He'd heard me talk about you a lot over the years and he's seen your social media too, if only to make fun of me for being a 'fanboy'." Ben made air quotes around the word but blushed and looked away.

"Josh is your brother? The other guy at the garage?"

"Yeah."

I sighed, scrubbing a hand over my face again. None of this was Ben's fault. It'd been plastering my face online for years. I'd also been widely outspoken about controversial issues, gaining me a huge amount of followers, even if some of them were trolls. Someone recognising me when I didn't want to be recognised was hardly unexpected, even if I'd hoped deactivating my social media accounts would make people forget I existed.

"This changes things," I said quietly.

Tonight, as we sat in my kitchen, we'd been two guys sharing Chinese food and talking, I felt like I could grow to trust Ben. He seemed so genuine and kind, so open with his feelings, no hidden agenda in sight. He made something inside me settle.

But now? Now that I knew he'd read my work, been following me online and knew more about me than I was ready to share, I felt my anxiety spike up. Maybe it wasn't fair, maybe I was being a dick about all this, but I needed some time to think this through.

I felt my walls rise up as I sat straighter in the chair, placing my elbows on the table. Looking him straight in the eyes I knew he'd felt it too. Ben raised a hand to stop whatever else I was about to say, his eyes darkening by regret and sadness.

"It's okay, I get it," he said, standing up. "I'll let myself out." He smiled weakly, pushing the chair back under the table. "Thank you for dinner..." Chewing on his bottom lip he paused, then added, "And I'm sorry. I should have said something before you invited me in your house."

He turned and left, and I didn't stop him.

CHAPTER EIGHT

The shrill ring of the bell startled me into spilling hot coffee on my hand and all over the counter. As I swore colourfully and reached for a paper towel, it rang again, driving me to nearly murderous rage. Who the fuck was ringing my bell at 9 AM?

Muttering curses under my breath I stalked to the door, not caring one bit I was wearing old – and now paint stained – sweats and a thread bare t-shirt with holes on the sleeve. I hadn't slept well the night before and the fatigue was adding to my exceedingly grumpy mood. The bell shrieked again just above my head as I reached for the handle, and I had to close my eyes and grind my teeth to stop myself from releasing a current of imaginative curses.

Mental note: disconnect the fucking bell the first chance I got.

I swung the door open with what I can imagine was a deadly glare. A teenage girl with bright red hair stood outside, her blue eyes fixed on me. She was wearing jean shorts and two, possibly three, differently coloured tank tops layered over one another.

She smiled at me. "Hi." She extended one hand while she clutched at a small package in the other. "I'm Rose." I glared at her hand but out of courtesy had to shake it. "I live across the road." She pointed to the house adjacent to Steve's.

"Great." I had two sets of neighbours and now I'd met them all. Hopefully their curiosity had been satisfied and they'd leave me the fuck alone. "Finn," I grunted.

Her smile wavered a bit, possibly because of my glower. I folded my hands across my chest and leaned against the door frame, waiting to see what she wanted.

"The postman dropped this off for you yesterday," she said, handing me the package. "Sorry I couldn't bring it to you last night but I was out with friends and mum was..."

"Thanks," I said, interrupting her and snagging the package out of her hand. Her eyes widened for a second, but then she narrowed them and glared back at me.

"I appreciate it." I added, taking a step back and preparing to close the door.

"You're new here," she said, taking a step forward towards me. "Right?"

She very well knew I was, why was she asking me stupid questions? It was too early in the morning for a chit-chat with a random teenager.

"How about a cup of coffee?" She said, smiling brightly.

I did not have the energy to try and find an excuse why I couldn't have coffee with her right now, so I sighed, hung my head and gestured her inside. She rewarded me with another bright smile and bounded towards the kitchen. I noticed she knew her way around the house as I followed her further inside.

"You're redecorating?" Rose asked, scanning my handiwork. I nodded and mumbled an agreement before switching the coffee machine back on. My own coffee had probably gone lukewarm by now so I might as well make a new cup for me too. "Old man Reed finally decided to sell?"

"Um, no," I said, glancing at her over my shoulder. She'd made herself comfortable in one of the extremely uncomfortable chairs. "I needed something to occupy my time and he cut me a deal on the rent if I do the place up."

Rose raised a sceptical eyebrow. "What do you do?"

"I'm currently unemployed," I said, pouring the freshly brewed coffee into two mugs. When I turned around she was watching me with a calculating stare much beyond her teenage years.

"How old are you?" I blurted. If she could be intrusive so could I, even if it meant lowering myself to the petty level of a teenager.

"Eighteen," she said, taking the mug I offered.

She didn't look eighteen. Maybe it was her make-up free face or her hair that hung loosely around her face, or her petite frame, but I'd never think the girl currently sitting at my kitchen table was technically an adult. The only thing that may have made me reconsider was her eyes. They held wisdom beyond her years, and a kind of melancholy even when she smiled.

"You?" She asked, hiding her smirk behind her cup as I glared at her.

"Twenty four."

"Wow, so you're a twenty-four-year-old handsome guy, unemployed, and renting an old house in the outskirts of a small town." She took a sip of coffee to emphasise the dramatic pause. The girl knew how to work an audience. "Not suspicious at all."

"Did you intrude on my morning to check if I'm a murderer?"

"I may have."

"All by yourself." I said, inserting a dramatic pause of my own. "In the outskirts of town. No witnesses. Alone in a potential murderer's house." Her eyes narrowed but a flicker of uncertainty in them told me she hadn't thought this all the way through. "Not very smart, Rose."

She rolled her eyes. "Steve said you're not a murderer."

"Well, then, I'm glad I'm the talk of the town." I inserted as much sarcasm in my statement as I could, my impatience firing up.

"Now, if you're satisfied with the results of your little quest, I have work to do."

She rolled her eyes again and I envied the amount of drama she could inject in such a small gesture. "Fine," she stood up, folding her thin arms. "You may not be a murderer, but you're rude. And kinda weird." She added, sizing me up with a critical stare.

"Whatever, Rose." I ushered her out of the kitchen and to the door. "I'll see you later."

She pranced out the door giving me a wicked smile over her shoulder.

"You will."

I'd had so much planned to do for the rest of the day, but I couldn't focus for shit. At first I was annoyed by Rose's unexpected and unwelcome visit, and dreaded the thought of her actually wanting to be friendly or something. I had to figure out how to ward her off next time. But then I couldn't stop thinking about Ben and what a dickhead I'd been to him. It was a little weird that he hadn't told me he knew who I was and had read my work *before* we had dinner together, but that didn't make him an opportunist. My gut was telling me Ben was a good guy, and my instincts were never wrong. I'd ignored my gut feeling way too many times in the past, but in the end it'd never lied to me.

I finished my cup of coffee and stood, casting a glare at the chair. Right. First thing on the to-do list for the day: buy new dining room chairs. I intended to spend a lot of time inside this house, and cook my own meals – or at least attempt it. I'd never cooked before in my life, but it couldn't be so difficult, could it? Mental note number two: buy cook books and groceries.

The package Rose had brought caught my eye while I was rinsing the cups in the sink. I knew it was from Aiden before I'd seen the return address. Nobody else knew my current address, not even Renee. We'd texted a bit since I moved but I wasn't ready to see her yet. I wasn't ready to stand in front of her and face my guilt and shame as she watched me with kind, unaccusing blue eyes. I wasn't ready to be forgiven yet.

Cutting the tape on the box, I smiled as I opened it and saw what was inside. Aiden had sent me chocolate, Irish moss pudding, his mum's salted caramel cookies, a stuffed Teddy to "warm my bed" as he'd written on the label attached to its ear, an apron with 'Mr Good Lookin is Cookin' written across the front, and a selection of exotic teas. I grinned as I remembered Aiden daring me to try a Mao Feng tea when we were in college. After I did, and admittedly quite liked it, it'd become our thing to try any odd tea flavour we came across. So far only kombucha and liquorice had made us both throw up, and fennel had made Aiden so drowsy he'd slept for fifteen hours. I'd nearly called an ambulance on him, scared the shit out of me.

Taking everything out of the box, and walking outside to the bins, I nearly threw it away in the recycling box before I noticed an envelope on the bottom. Inside was a fridge magnet, a drawing of a typewriter on it, and the words 'Just my typo'. It was probably something you could buy in any gift shop and shouldn't have made me rapidly blink tears away, but it did. And then I saw what Aiden had written on a piece of paper.

Isn't it time you found your words again?

A memory so vivid burst behind my eyelids as I closed my eyes.

"What happens when I run out of words, Aiden?" I'd asked.

"I don't think that'll ever happen." Aiden'd said, sitting down on the sofa next to me and closing the laptop on my lap. "Words are not a finite number you carry inside you. They're something you search for and eventually find. So yeah, sometimes you may have trouble digging them out, but other times they will be flying freely around you and all you have to do is reach out and grab them."

I'd taken his words quite literally; I'd imagined myself digging a huge hole in the dry dirt only to find a couple of scattered letters on the bottom, and then a flock of birds, their bodies made of words, flew all around me, like a hurricane, the wind from their wings blowing my hair and my clothes in all directions. "And sometimes," Aiden'd continued, placing a hand on my arm to anchor me back to reality. "They'll be like raw clay you have to mould and shape and reshape before it's ready for baking." He'd winked at me and smiled, and in that moment I'd believed him.

I opened my eyes, clutching the magnet and the note so hard my knuckles had gone white. My eyes stung and my heart felt heavy and bruised, my lungs suddenly unable to get enough air in. Throwing the box in the bin, I turned on my heel and stomped back inside the house, slamming the door behind me.

There was no fucking way I'd be able to fit six dining room chairs in my car, even if they were flat-packed. The guy who'd helped me wheel the huge trolley through the car park knew it too. He glanced at the car, then at the bulky boxes piled on the trolley, then at me, raising an eyebrow and folding his arms with a smirk, as if thinking, *Go on, then, I really want to see how you'll manage that.*

"Do you offer a delivery service?" I asked, running a hand through my new, short hair. I hadn't quite buzzed it all off like Aiden, but it was shorter than I'd ever had it, and still felt a little weird when I ran my hand through it.

"We do." He didn't move, as if daring me to at least give it a try. I was certain he'd be no help at all, but instead take out his phone and film me trying to stuff six furniture boxes in the boot of my sports car. I could probably manage one, two at the most, and probably a couple on the back seat but the thought of scratching the leather with the rough cardboard made me shudder.

"Alright, then," I said, clicking the remote and locking the car after depositing the smaller bags inside. "I'd like to have the chairs delivered as soon as possible, please."

The guy – Martin, as his name tag said – glanced at his watch.

"It's half an hour till closing on a Friday, mate," he said with a sigh. "The best we can do is Monday."

Great. Fantastic.

I couldn't even be bothered to argue, or even bribe him. I'd had an exhausting day shopping for kitchen stuff and bathroom stuff and cooking books and all other kinds of crap. All I wanted to do was go home, fall in bed, and order a takeaway.

"That's fine," I said, walking past him back towards the shop to fill in the paperwork. "Can I at least have them delivered first thing in the morning on Monday?" I'd never put together any flat-packed furniture and I had a feeling it may take me a while to get the hang of it, but for some irrational reason it'd become very important to me that I eat my dinner Monday night sitting in that damn chair.

"We don't do time slots. It could be any time between eight and six," the guy said as he wheeled the trolley back towards the shop.

Of course. It would have been too easy otherwise.

Turning into a quiet, residential street I parked the car and turned off the engine. Ben's garage was close by and I knew they closed at six, so I wanted to get there before Ben left for the day. I wanted to talk to him, but not there. His dad and his brother seemed alright, but I was too exhausted to keep track of anyone giving me the side eye and judging me. Even though Ben gave me a feeling he was a nice guy, I didn't know him. I didn't know what he'd said to his family about me or how they were going to react to me prancing inside the garage and demanding to talk to Ben.

My heart started pounding faster as I rehearsed what I was going to say in my head. I didn't know why it was so important to me that Ben didn't think of me as an arrogant bastard but it was, and the only way to do that was to be sincere. Clamming up and sarcastic, sometimes outright cruel, remarks were my defence mechanism, nurtured by years of having to deal with my mother, but I didn't want to be like that anymore. I wanted to trust people; I wanted to have relationships where I could let my guard down and be myself.

The glowing numbers on the dashboard reminded me it was time to go. I hadn't been this nervous since submitting my manuscript to an agent for the first time. I'd entirely forgotten what it felt like to have your heart racing and stomach turning in anticipation of something that could go disastrously wrong.

Five minutes before the garage was about to close, I parked the car in front, leaving the engine running. I intended to lurk around until Ben showed up instead of going inside like a normal person.

Not a minute later I saw Ben walking out, his brother right behind him. Ben had his hands in his pockets and his head bent as if he was listening intently to what his brother was telling him. Josh was talking animatedly, gesturing with his hands, touching Ben's shoulder from time to time as if to get his attention.

I sat in my car, watching them, my heart pounding as I waited for Ben to raise his head and see me. He did, just as Josh laughed loudly, clutching Ben's upper arm. Our eyes met and I flashed my lights at him, hoping he'd understand I wanted him to come over. Josh saw me too, his smile disappearing as he glared at me.

Ben walked towards me after saying something to his brother over his shoulder. Josh kept glowering with a frown, even as Ben climbed in my passenger seat, but he was in his car and speeding away before Ben'd even closed the door.

"Hi," I said, glancing at Ben, trying to judge his mood.

"Hi." He didn't look at me as he replied, but I didn't sense any hostility in his body language. He'd readily come to my car when he'd seen me so he couldn't be upset with me, right?

"Can we talk?"

"Yeah," he said with a casual shrug, still not looking at me.

"I don't like how we left things off last night and wanted a chance to explain."

That got his attention. He turned to look at me, eyes wide.

"I find it hard to trust people," I said, holding his gaze. "And my first instinct when I feel even slightly threatened is to shut people out completely."

Ben licked his lips, nodding as if things started to make a bit more sense in his head.

"But I'm working on that. Because it can get very lonely when you think everyone's out there to get you, and you shut people out before you've given them a chance." It was what Renee had always told me and I'd rolled my eyes at her.

Ben was staring at me with those big, green eyes, his dark eyelashes lowering as he glanced at my lips for merely a second before looking away.

"So..." I fumbled, feeling my cheeks flush. "I guess I'm trying to say I'm sorry for how I reacted last night, and I hope we can be friends. I could use a friend right now."

I felt exposed and vulnerable as I'd never felt before, and while it was scary and uncomfortable, and I really needed Ben to say something before I exploded, I also welcomed this new feeling. I'd come here to try and become a better person, and once my arrogance was stripped away, I had very little left to protect me.

"And if that friend is the best mechanic in town, that's just a bonus," I said with a casual shrug, a smile playing on my lips as

Ben turned to face me again. He was smiling too, and my stomach did a weird fluttering thing I didn't care for.

"Best mechanic in town, eh?"

"Yeah. It's a lucky coincidence I drive a rubbish sports car, and a mechanic friend would be a godsend."

"A very lucky coincidence."

We were both grinning like morons by that point, my chest expanding with relief.

CHAPTER NINE

I put Aiden's magnet on the fridge. Every time I glanced at it something akin to pain sliced through my heart, and yet I didn't remove it. As I sipped my coffee sitting in the uncomfortable chair, I stared at the magnet, Aiden's words repeating on a loop in my head.

It wasn't like I didn't have stories to tell. There was a spiderweb full of untold stories in my head, but the very idea of sitting down in front of my laptop and loading the empty page terrified me. Just thinking about it made my anxiety spike up, a craving for something, anything, to dull the jittery feeling forcing its way inside my brain.

I sipped some more lukewarm coffee, my mind delving into places I didn't want it to go and yet unable to stop. How difficult would it be to find some prescription pills here, or even some weed? I didn't know anyone local who could hook me up, but I was sure a quick google search could point me in the right direction. Or, I could text one of my mates and ask... London was just about an hour drive from here, it wasn't like I was in Scotland.

The doorbell's shrill ring jolted me out of my cancerous thoughts. I sat there, shaking so bad I couldn't hold the mug in my hands. The dangerous thoughts had scattered, but the uneasy feeling remained.

What if I hadn't been interrupted? How far would I have gone if there was nobody to stop me? What about next time?

The doorbell rang again, more insistently this time, so I got up on shaky legs and walked to the front door. Opening it with a forceful swing, I saw Rose standing on my threshold, holding a small, fluffy dog, and smiling widely at me as if I was the best thing she'd seen all day.

"I thought you said I was weird and rude," I said with confidence I didn't feel inside. "What are you doing here then?"

Her smile didn't falter as if she'd expected me to be a dickhead.

"Wanna come for a walk?" She asked pleasantly.

"No."

"Come on," she coaxed. "The weather is gorgeous and I think you can use some sun." I only raised an eyebrow and folded my arms. Why was this teenager making friends with me? "I'll show you something." She smiled wickedly.

"What?"

"Come and see." Her dog barked once at me as if sticking up for his – her? – owner.

Truth was, I could really use a walk. Especially after what'd just happened in the kitchen. And a part of me was glad Rose had come round to get me, but I didn't intend to tell her any of that, or she might get the idea that I liked her.

"Fine. Let me put my shoes on," I said, walking back inside the house but leaving the door open.

"And sun screen," she called after me.

I was tempted to tell her to fuck off, but I was pretty sure that wasn't how you were supposed to talk to teenagers.

"What's his name?" I asked, jerking my chin at the dog.

"It's a girl," Rose said, casting a loving glance at the dog. "Eren."

I gave her a puzzled look. "Eren? But it's a girl?"

Rose looked at me with narrowed eyes. "You watch Attack on Titan?"

"Yeah."

She narrowed her eyes at me, but then nodded her approval, and said, "Yes, it's a girl named after my favourite male character. I refuse to conform to society's stupid gender roles." She kicked a pebble with her shoe, sending it flying.

Eren was a surprisingly well-behaved shorkie. She rarely strayed from Rose's side and managed to trot around every puddle without Rose telling her. I watched her suspiciously, certain she was planning something because that wasn't normal dog behaviour. I was no expert but every dog I've ever met couldn't wait to roll around in the biggest and smelliest pile of shit they could find.

Rose led me to the forest I always saw from my bedroom window. It wasn't as far away as it seemed, especially after Rose's sneaky shortcut. Inside, under the thick shade of the trees, the relief I felt from the sticky June heat was instant. I even shivered a little as we walked along a well-trodden path, the sun rays barely managing to slip between the leaves.

"Are you dating Ben Goodwin?" Rose asked, without any preamble, just as I was starting to enjoy the peace and quiet of the forest.

"Why would you even ask me that?"

"Because I saw him at your house the other day, and then you two looked awfully cosy at Marco's last night," she said, glancing at me with a smirk I found very annoying.

We'd gone for a cup of coffee – and as it turned out, a slice of tiramisu – after our talk in the car, and it'd been fun. Ben was very easy-going and impossible to dislike, unlike myself. The few times I'd been in his company I'd felt relaxed as I'd never before been in my life, as if somehow he'd managed to quiet the voices inside me without even trying. Knowing someone had intruded on that, watched us, possibly even judged us, made me uneasy.

I frowned but kept my voice light. "Now who's the creepy stalker?"

She expertly rolled her eyes, then turned around to face me, walking backwards.

"I just happened to be in the area."

"Both times?"

"Yeah." She shrugged one shoulder, her gaze steady on mine, still demanding answers.

"Are we seriously having this conversation right now?" My annoyance kept spiking up to a point where I was unable to keep it from creeping in my tone.

This was one of the major issues I'd had about moving to a small town. I hated people sticking their nose in my business, and I hated that they thought it was okay. As if I owed anyone any explanation.

"Ben's a good guy," Rose said, her eyes softening. She turned around again, walking shoulder to shoulder with me. "He went to school with my sister. She had a major crush on him, and was devastated when he turned her down." Eren found something on the ground and barked at it once, then nudged it with her paw before losing interest. Rose watched her, but seemed distracted. "Maya, my sister, said he didn't date much in school, turned everyone down, not just her, but I never knew if that was true or she just wanted to make herself feel better."

I wasn't sure why she was telling me this. I was still hung up on the fact that she'd effectively spied on us and was demanding to know about my personal life, and I couldn't move past that so easily.

"Look, Rose, I don't mean to be rude, but I'm not comfortable talking about my personal life with someone I'd just met. And I'd appreciate it if you stop spying on me."

I may have sounded a bit testier than I'd meant, but I couldn't help it. To her credit, Rose didn't seem to take offense. She studied me for a few seconds, but then she simply nodded and we kept walking in silence for a while.

The soothing sounds of the forest and the cool breeze helped me relax again, and as we walked I tried to empty my mind of everything, and just *be*. I tried to remember the relaxation and meditation techniques a yoga instructor had tried to teach Aiden and me after an ill-advised New Year's resolution to take up yoga. The poor guy had been so serious about the lessons while Aiden and I kept giggling as we sat cross-legged on the floor, emptying our minds.

"What are you thinking about?" Rose's voice brought me out of my thoughts and back to the moment. I must have looked confused because she shook her head a little and said, "You were smiling just now. What were you thinking about?"

"Yoga," I said, injecting as much finality in the word as I could muster.

"Here," Rose said, grabbing hold of my wrist and pulling me through a thick bush. The branches scratched at my bare arms and legs, and I let out a few curses.

"What the fuck, Rose? A bit of warning before you pull me into the bushes next time?" I dusted off a few leaves from my t-shirt and looked at my legs, wincing. The red scratches looked striking against my pale skin. And one on my arm was even starting to bleed.

"Sorry, forgot you've never been in the wilderness before." She didn't sound sorry at all and when I looked at her, she was smiling.

I bit back the words that came to mind before I accidentally said something I would have to apologise for later.

Eren barked impatiently at us, and I looked around to see where she was. We stood in a small, unkempt clearing, the grass and wild flowers growing freely without any human intervention.

There was no clear path, but I followed Rose as she started walking confidently after her dog. The sound of running water reached my ears and grew louder as we walked towards it, Rose turning around every few seconds to check if I was following.

"The bushes here are not as thick, but you might want to be careful," she said before disappearing into another damn bush.

"For fuck's sake! Can't we follow a path like civilised people?" I sighed loudly, hoping she'd hear me from behind the bushes, and bent to walk through them.

It was true, the branches weren't as thick as before, and with careful manoeuvring I managed to walk through without too much trouble. On the other side, Rose was sitting on the shore of a small stream, taking her shoes off. Eren was already jumping excitedly in the water, barking happily at Rose.

"I'm coming, jeez, patience," Rose scolded her bouncing dog, but I could hear the smile in her voice.

The thought of dipping my feet in the cold water seemed refreshing, so I took my shoes off as I reached the stream and joined them. The water barely reached my calves and was colder than I expected. A shiver ran through my body at the first contact, but I soon got used to it and managed to relax. Rose and Eren kept running around, playing and splashing, Rose squealing happily as her dog barked and shook her wet fur.

I stood there, smiling like an idiot despite myself, watching them play. Until Rose eyed me with a mischievous sparkle in her eye I didn't care for, and kicked water in my direction, splashing the whole front of my t-shirt.

Now, it was war.

My clothes were mostly dry by the time we got back. Seemed like playing in the stream had loosened us both, and Rose kept chatting all the way back, telling me bits of information about the town and its population I didn't really need to hear, or cared about. But instead of getting all annoyed about it, I let her voice drift around me, and I even let myself enjoy some of the gossip about people I didn't know. Once upon a time it'd been a hobby of mine to watch people and figure out why they behaved a certain way, or come up with back stories about strangers I saw on the street; other times I'd been delighted to listen to stories about strangers' lives, fuelling my own imagination. But that had been a long time ago, it seemed. Nowadays I got frustrated about every little thing, not seeing the point in any of it.

Rose stopped in front of her house and picked up Eren. She faced me with a bright smile and said, "Thanks, Finn. I had fun today." She used her dog's paw to wave at me and I had to bite my lip against a smile. I didn't want to give her the impression that I found that dog cute in any way, because I certainly didn't.

"Me too," I said, shoved my hands in my pockets and walked back to my house.

CHAPTER TEN

On my way back from the supermarket, my car gave me the perfect excuse to call Ben again. I *wanted* to call him, and I'd been racking my brain for any reason other than just wanting to hang out with him, when the service light lit up on the dashboard.

"Thanks, baby," I said, caressing the steering wheel and grinning like an idiot.

I snapped a quick photo of the offending light and texted it to him. When he didn't respond straight away, I stashed the phone in my pocket and went to unload the grocery bags. I soon realised I might have overestimated the capacity of the fridge. Just as I was playing Tetris with the vegetables, trying to fit them all in the 'keep fresh' drawer, my phone rang. Ben's name flashed on the screen and I tried to keep the smile from my voice as I answered.

"Hey," I said, leaning against the kitchen counter, trying to sound cool. "I think my car likes you a bit too much. She'd do anything to see you again."

Ben laughed softly. "I don't mind. I like her, too. A lot."

His voice was tickling all my senses. Closing my eyes, I let myself enjoy the deep, tender tones, imagining it falling lower, turning deeper as Ben whispered filthy things in my ear.

I inhaled sharply, snapping my eyes open and adjusting my dick in my jeans.

"Why don't you bring her round Monday morning?" Ben was saying when I started paying attention to the actual words again. "I had someone booked for an engine check but Josh can take that, and I'll service your car. Should be ready before the end of the day."

"Yeah, sure, sounds good," I said, clearing my throat. Something started beeping close to me, startling me. Looking around I saw I'd forgotten to close the fridge door when Ben'd called. I pushed it firmly closed, then leaned against it.

I was aware I should probably thank him and end the call, but dammit, the whole point was to find a reason to see him again. Today, not on Monday. Any rational person would have realised Ben wasn't working on a Saturday afternoon, but rationality wasn't my strongest quality.

"Is there... anything else?" I could picture the slight frown that formed on his face in that little pause he made. I could also hear quiet music in the background, and imagined Ben sprawled on his sofa, wearing comfortable sweats and an old t-shirt, arm folded under his head as he held the phone with the other.

I was probably completely wrong and he could be with someone else right now and I was being an annoying asshole, calling him about work on the weekend. But, I wanted to see him so bad, my mouth was saying the words before I changed my mind.

"What are you doing right now?" I asked in a single rush of breath. Closing my eyes with embarrassment I thanked the universe he couldn't see me right now as I lightly thumped my head against the fridge.

"Not much," he said, seemingly unbothered by my question. "Reading," he added.

"Want to hang out?" I bit my lip, feeling incredibly stupid for some reason. I had no idea why he was intimidating me so much. "I don't have much going on either."

Ben chuckled softly. "There isn't much going on in Ten Mile Bottom, even on the weekends. You'll have to come down to Cambridge if you want to have some fun."

"Come down? Is that where you are?"

"Yeah. My flat's here," Ben said and I heard some rustling as if he was moving.

"You drive to Ten Mile Bottom every day? Isn't it supposed to be the other way around? Live in the quiet, small town and drive to the city for work?"

He chuckled again and I barely resisted closing my eyes and imagining doing dirty things to him again.

"Yeah, but I don't like doing anything the conventional way." He paused for longer than I liked, and I realised he never really answered my question. "Feel like driving down here?"

"Yeah, I guess." My nonchalance needed some work. I cleared my throat again. "Where do you want to meet?"

"Come over to my place, you can park here and we can walk if we decide to go out. Parking in the city centre is a nightmare, especially on a Saturday."

My heart started beating fast the moment he asked me to go to his flat, and nearly exploded when he suggested we might not even leave it. I couldn't imagine anything more tempting than spending the evening alone with Ben, not in some noisy pub, but at his place.

He texted me his address shortly after we hung up. I saved it and pulled up the navigation app. It estimated I should be there in about forty minutes. Taking a shower and getting dressed shouldn't take me more than twenty minutes, so I'd see Ben in about an hour.

I smiled and hurried up the stairs with an extra spring in my step.

Ben looked pretty much as I'd imagined him before – a comfortable pair of sweat pants, an old t-shirt and barefoot. Only, he had a tea towel draped on his shoulder and was holding an oven mitt. He'd tried to tame his unruly hair with an elastic band, but several wavy strands had slipped the knot on his head.

"Hey," he said, waving me in as he hurried back inside. I walked in, toeing off my shoes and closing the door. "Sorry, I have to make sure I stir the sauce or it'll burn." He threw me a grin over his shoulder as I walked into the kitchen.

The fragrant aromas of basil, oregano and garlic drifted from the stove and my mouth watered.

"You shouldn't have cooked," I said, placing the bottle of wine I'd grabbed on the way on the table and pulled up a chair. "We could have gone out. I hate putting you through all this trouble."

"It's no trouble." He removed the pot from the stove and placed it on a wooden chopping board on the counter. "It's just spaghetti." He turned to fully face me and pointed at the bottle of wine I'd place on the table "Would you like some wine? I don't drink but I can get you a glass."

"No, that's fine, I don't drink either." I felt like an idiot bringing the bottle when I didn't know Ben that well. He didn't seem bothered by it, but a shadow passed over his bright eyes when he'd mentioned he didn't drink.

Ben swiped the bottle from the table and put it in a cupboard above the stove. "I can always use it for cooking," he threw over his shoulder with a grin, as if sensing my discomfort.

He went back to stirring the sauce, and I became antsy to find something to do.

Ben ran a hand through his messy hair, turning to look at me. "Do you mind if we stay here? I don't really feel like going out."

"Sure." I shrugged as if it wasn't a big deal when in fact I was overjoyed I wouldn't have to face a crowded restaurant or a pub. Staying in with Ben, just the two of us, was my idea of heaven right now. "Can I help?"

"The sauce is ready, the pasta is boiling," he said, pointing at another pot on the stove. "I guess all that's left is a salad."

I was hopeless in the kitchen, but I was willing to learn, and besides, even I couldn't mess up chopping a few vegetables.

"Alright, I can do that."

Ben opened the fridge and started taking out vegetables for the salad, placing them on the counter. I went to stand next to him, waiting. When he was done, he pointed at the cupboard and drawers where he stored the chopping boards, bowls, knifes and condiments, and left me to it, going back to the stove to stir the pasta.

We worked side by side for a while, bumping shoulders as we had to pass around each other or stretch to get something. Ben's kitchen wasn't huge but the space was utilised well so it didn't feel cramped. The pastel green cupboards and cream counters gave it a cosy feel, and the small dining area added to its appeal. I didn't get how people could always eat standing up, bent over the counter or, even worse, holding a plate while sitting on the sofa in front of the TV. I hated that. When I mentioned it to Ben, he nodded vigorously.

"My mum would smack me over the head of she saw me balancing a full plate on my knees while wrestling with the remote," he said with a fond smile. "Meal times in our house are always savoured, usually with family and friends. When I was growing up we'd always eat dinner together, no TV or phones allowed. If the house phone rang my parents would ignore it and call back later. Some of the fondest memories of my childhood are around that dining table, or in the kitchen. To this day Mum and Dad always have dinner together, talking about their day or the latest family gossip."

"Did your mum teach you how to cook?" I asked, jerking my chin towards the pasta he was expertly stirring into the sauce.

"She did, both me and Josh. She says cooking is a basic skill, and no child of hers will be eating take-away every night or depending on other people to cook for them."

I envied the warm smile on Ben's face as he talked about his mother.

"Your mum sounds awesome," I said, mixing the salad with the dressing I'd poured over it.

"She really is."

I felt like a black hole opened in the pit of my stomach, ready to expand and swallow me whole. Its darkness clouded my mind, feeding me memories I wished I could forget. My mother screaming at my father that he was late for dinner, again; my father offering to help with the dishes, albeit reluctantly, and mum cutting him off, saying he wouldn't do it properly and she'd have to do it all over again; Renee and I waking up early on Mother's Day to surprise her with breakfast, and of course making a mess because Renee wasn't even tall enough to reach the counter, and being yelled at for it, the breakfast dumped in the trash because the toast was burned and the eggs were runny and mother didn't like them like that and we should know better...

"Finn?" Ben's voice was closer than I expected, startling me. I must have spaced out for longer than I thought because it didn't seem like that was the first time he'd called my name. "Are you alright?" His face was right in front of me, worry darkening his green eyes.

I wanted nothing more than to cut the few inches between us and kiss the breath out of him, pull him close and inhale his scent, run a hand through that messy hair. My eyes lowered to his lips, just for a second, but it was enough to make Ben frown.

"I'm fine," I said in a rush, taking a step back and putting my hands apologetically in front of me. I'd rather die than have him frown at me, or, even worse, pity me. "I have a habit of spacing out sometimes. Comes with the job." I grinned at him, hoping he'd believe me and we can go back to chatting and hanging out as if I was a normal person.

"I suppose it does," he said, choosing to believe me.

We brought the food to the table and sat down to eat, Ben streaming quiet music on his phone. It took me a few minutes to fully relax again, though. There was something in Ben's presence that calmed the voices in my head and made everything around me quiet. I couldn't resist the pull of that serene silence even if I wanted to.

"You know what would feel so good right now?" Ben asked, after we finished our meal and tidied up the kitchen together. I had a dozen answers to that question that involved both of us naked and sweaty, but I knew it wasn't what Ben was implying. "Ice-cream," he said when I shook my head.

He pulled out four different tubs of ice-cream from the freezer, as well as strawberry sauce, marshmallows, chocolate buttons and biscuits, and displayed them on the counter with flourish. Grabbing two bowls from the overhead cupboard, and a couple of spoons, he announced with a boyish grin,

"Dig in."

God, but I wanted him. "Um, okay?" I said, holding awkwardly the spoon and bowl he'd handed me.

Ben started scooping ice-cream in his bowl, then pouring chocolate sauce over it with childish glee. I followed his example which made me feel like a kid again too, but I refused to give in to the urge to look over my shoulder, fearing my mother would scold me for the mess or for eating too much sugar that late in the evening. Instead, I inched closer to Ben, letting my guard down, just for a little while. He didn't move away, but met my eyes and winked, licking his spoon clean before sticking it in the huge pile of the ice-cream concoction he'd made.

"You need more marshmallows," he told me, scooping some from the bag and dumping them in my bowl.

"I'd really like to leave here tonight diabetes-free, if you don't mind," I said, but didn't pick the marshmallows off my ice-cream.

Ben laughed, then started putting everything away before the ice-cream had melted. He gestured for me to follow him as he headed out of the kitchen and into the living room. Much like the kitchen, Ben's living room was small, but cosy. Pastel colours dominated the decor, with a few intense accents like the dark red rug in front of the sofa, and the navy curtains. Pictures of his family hung on the walls, as well as a few beautiful abstract paintings. One in particular caught my eye and I moved closer to take a better look. The striking black lines on a silver background didn't resemble anything I could put a name on, but they made me feel melancholic for some reason.

Ben'd walked over, standing right behind me. I could feel his body heat through my thin t-shirt, his scent surrounding me, not letting me forget how attracted to him I was.

"Josh made that," Ben said, his breath brushing the skin on my neck.

I turned to face him, surprised. I didn't really know his brother but the one time I'd seen him, he hadn't looked like an artist at all.

"Really?" I said, unable to hide my surprise.

"Yeah." Ben's green eyes twinkled with mirth. We were standing so close I could see the gold specks in them, and could appreciate his long, dark eyelashes even more. "He looks like a brute, but the truth is he's a gentle artist."

Ben smiled widely at his own comment. I wanted nothing more than to pull him close and kiss that smile away. I really needed to curb my lust for the guy before I'd ruined whatever we had here. He hadn't made a single flirtatious comment all night, and I was starting to feel like a creep, perving on him all the time.

TEN MILE BOTTOM

I took a step back. "The ice-cream is probably melting," I said, lamely, and headed to the sofa. Ben followed, turning on the TV on low volume.

It was more of a background noise as we talked and ate our huge dessert. He made me laugh more than I ever remember laughing, making me melt into the sofa cushions. It was probably irrational, but I felt safe in Ben's apartment, even though I was here for the first time. All too soon, the ice-cream was eaten and it was getting pretty late. I knew I had to go soon, but I didn't want to. Leaving this small, cosy apartment and Ben's presence seemed like torture right now.

The ring of Ben's phone felt like a loud, ugly stain on our perfect evening. I winced as it went off on the coffee table, feeling as if I was being violently jerked back to reality.

Ben picked up, and I could hear loud music coming from the other end of the call. Soon, it quieted down as if the person calling had moved away from it. It felt weird for me to eavesdrop on his conversation, even if Ben hadn't moved away, so I picked up the empty bowls and took them to the kitchen sink. I rinsed them and placed them on the drainer, hoping I'd given Ben enough time to finish his call.

"Ugh, I really can't be bothered, mate," Ben was saying as I walked back into the living room. "I know, but he won't even notice I'm not there!" He paused, listening. I sat back down next to him, thinking it would be more uncomfortable if I lurked in the doorway. "Alright, I guess..." He said with a heavy sigh. I busied myself with changing the TV channels. "Fine. I'll be there in about an hour."

Ben ended the call and my stomach plummeted. He'd agreed to go out with his friends, who were part of his world, unlike me. It meant the end of our cosy cocoon.

"My mates are celebrating Marc's promotion and apparently can't do without me," Ben said, rolling his eyes when I looked at him. "Feel like going out?"

I appreciated the invitation but my mood had already suffered a deadly blow. I didn't want to go to some club with people I didn't know, possibly watching everyone as they got drunk – or worse – and had to fight the urge to get plastered, all the while sharing Ben's attention with his friends. In fact, it was the last thing I wanted to do right now.

"Nah, I'm pretty tired, I think I'm going to head home," I said, managing a weak smile. "Thanks for tonight. I had a good time."

Ben looked disappointed that I wouldn't be joining him, but didn't try to convince me to go. He saw me to the door, not closing it until I climbed into my car and turned the engine on. With a wave, I sped away, not letting myself overthink and overanalyse every little thing that had happened tonight. All I wanted was my bed and to be consumed by a dreamless slumber. Hopefully, that would be enough to shut my overactive mind, at least for the night.

CHAPTER ELEVEN

Ben came to pick up my car bright and early on Monday morning. Hearing the doorbell, I rolled out of bed with a grunt. I'd forgotten he'd offered to come get the car and leave his in the driveway instead of me having to get a taxi back and forth.

No wonder it'd slipped my mind. I'd spent the entire day yesterday with my phone turned off, hiding from the world and feeling sorry for myself. I'd slept nearly the entire day and yet I still felt like shit this morning.

I needed to piss, badly, so I opted for a quick trip to the bathroom before opening the door, hoping that splashing my face with cold water would make me feel half-decent. It did not.

When I opened the door, Ben was standing a few feet away, holding his phone to his ear.

"Oh, hey," he said, putting it back in his pocket. "I was just about to climb through the window to check if you're alive." He pointed to the open window on the second floor and grinned.

Unlike me, he looked rested and put together in blue jeans and a V-neck black t-shirt, hair still a bit damp.

"Had a late night last night," I said, my voice hoarse as I hadn't talked in a while. Ben frowned, but his gaze was more concerned than angry. I cleared my throat.

"Here," I said, handing him the keys. "Take care of my baby." I tried to smile and felt my lips pull uncomfortably, the skin so dry it was nearly painful.

"Of course." He took the keys, still studying me, probably trying to figure out what the hell had happened between Saturday and now.

Good luck, mate. I'm still trying to figure it out myself.

"You can bring her round after you're done for the day," I said when he didn't immediately turn to leave. "I don't really need the car today, I'm waiting for a delivery."

Ben nodded and turned to leave. I closed the door before he'd even unlocked the car.

Fuck, I was a mess. My chest hurt like someone had stomped on me, and I didn't know why. Anger, sadness and insecurity were fighting for dominance in my head, tearing me apart. Really soon, the craving for something to dull the pain would appear and I didn't know if I was strong enough to resist it.

But I had to be.

I had to be.

I had to be!

I was not going back to being how I was. To hurting the few people I loved. To being a worthless piece of shit, only thinking about his next hit.

Determination rose in me, overriding everything else as I climbed the stairs back to my bedroom, threw the clothes I'd slept in in the laundry bin and headed for the bathroom.

After a quick shower, shave, and a light breakfast, I was ready to throw myself into work and not think about anything else for a while. The hardwood floors needed a thorough clean and a new coat of varnish, so my goal for the day was to do at least two rooms. Hopefully, the chairs would arrive at some point while I was doing that and I'd have something else to occupy me till the end of the day.

Selecting a new audiobook I'd bought and sticking my ear buds in, I started working. The repetitive manual labour and the deep voice of the narrator in my ears helped me quiet my thoughts, and finally relax.

It would have been perfect if it wasn't so damn hot. I hated the sticky British summer, especially when there was no air-conditioning in the house, or a nice pool to dive in. At this point I'd take a walk in the woods and a dip in the stream, but unfortunately I had to wait for the fucking delivery.

Wiping the sweat running down my face with the bottom of my t-shirt, I paused the audiobook and removed the ear buds. I needed a break and something cold to drink.

I was chugging a cold bottle of water down when my phone rang from the other room where I'd left it. I hurried to get it, smiling when I saw Renee's picture and name flashing on the screen.

"Hey, Sis," I said, flopping down on the sofa with a heavy sigh. "What's up?"

"I'm going to kill someone before this day is over," Renee said without any heat in her voice.

I laughed and asked what had gotten her so riled up. She complained about her 'illiterate colleagues' for a solid fifteen minutes before she ran out of steam. I was used to listening to that rant. Renee was a social worker, and even though she liked the job itself, she loathed some of the people she had to work with. If it was me I'd have quit a long time ago, but Renee was a fighter. She'd stick by something she believed in even if it tore her apart.

"I can use a bit of a break in the countryside," she said and I could hear the smirk in her voice.

"I can send you a link for this amazing little cottage we went to last year."

"Finn!" Renee exclaimed, exasperated. "This is getting ridiculous. You can't hide from us till the end of time."

"Us?"

"Me and Mum!"

"So you're, what, a team now?" I knew I sounded childishly defensive, but if Renee took my mother's side on anything it'd kill me.

"Don't be like that," she said, her voice softer. "If you're not ready to see Mum yet that's fine, but please let me come visit you. I miss you, Finn."

I didn't know what to say. I missed her, too, more than I was willing to admit. I didn't trust my voice to speak so the silence stretched until Renee said,

"Finn, it wasn't your fault. I don't blame you. Luis doesn't blame you. It was meant to happen and it would have, one way or another."

I shifted on the sofa, my back starting to hurt from all the scrubbing I'd done, and winced. "Do you understand that?" Renee asked, the words clipped and clear as if she was speaking to a wayward child.

"It's not about that," I lied. "I just want to finish working on the house. There's literally nowhere for you to sleep right now."

"We'll get a hotel nearby."

I sighed. When she got something into her head she was like a bulldog.

"How about you all come for my birthday?" I said, running my tongue over my teeth, before adding, "Mum, too."

Renee perked up. "Yeah? You mean it?"

"I do. It's five weeks away so hopefully I'll have plenty of time to get the house in shape. We'll have a barbeque in the garden and everything. You can stay for the weekend if you want."

"I'd love that!" Renee exclaimed.

TEN MILE BOTTOM

Renee's mood improved considerably after that and we chatted some more, gossiping about mutual acquaintances. I told her about Steve and Ruby, and about Rose and her dog.

I didn't tell her about Ben. Somehow that felt too important to share, as if talking about it would break the fragile friendship we had, killing any chances of it becoming anything more.

Not that it stood any chances right now. I didn't even know if Ben was into guys at all. I'd definitely picked up some interest from him when we were together but I might have misread him.

We said our goodbyes, promising to talk again soon. With a heavy sigh I stood up, stretched my arms over my head, my spine popping, and headed back to the spare bedroom. I had floors to varnish.

The chairs arrived as I was putting the lasagne in the oven. I'd varnished the floors and with nothing left to do I'd decided to give my new cooking book a go. Lasagne seemed very easy and straightforward, so that was what I went for. Making it hadn't been a complete disaster, except for burning the sauce and having to start over, but if it tasted good was a whole new story.

The delivery men dumped the six big boxes in the middle of my entryway and left. I crossed my arms and stared at them, wondering what on earth I'd been thinking when I'd decided I could put these together. I didn't even have any tools. Well, apart from a screwdriver, a hammer, and a measuring tape. Even if I did, I had no idea how to use them.

As if summoned by my helplessness, Ben appeared round the corner, driving my car smoothly into the driveway.

"Hi," he said, getting out of the car.

I waved at him, silently battling with myself whether I should ask him for help. I didn't want to seem like a complete loser who couldn't even do the simplest of things, but I also really wanted my new chairs to be put together properly and not fall apart as soon as someone sat on them.

"What's this?" Ben asked, staring at the boxes.

"My new kitchen chairs."

Ben handed me the keys to my car with a smile. "Why are you staring at them as if they'd personally offended you?"

I ignored his question, not willing to own up to my helplessness just yet, and jerked my chin towards the car. "All good?"

"Yeah, everything seems fine."

"Come on in, I'll go grab my wallet and pay you."

Ben walked in, carefully stepping around the boxes, and followed me into the kitchen. I paid him for the car service – for which I still thought he was undercharging me considering I last paid twice that much in London – but I didn't feel like arguing right now.

"Smells good. You cooking?" Ben said with a raised eyebrow.

"Trying to," I said, pointing at the cooking book. "I'm still learning."

Ben grinned at me, his boyish smile so charming I couldn't help but return it.

"You need some help with those chairs?" He stuck his thumb in the direction of the boxes, once again knowing what I needed before I'd even said it.

"I guess, if you have nothing better to do."

Ben hummed, following behind me as I went to grab one of the boxes.

"How do we always end up having dinner together?" Ben asked as I placed a plate in front of him. His teasing grin went straight to my cock.

"Fate," I said with a shrug. Ben shook his head a little, but his dimpled grin stayed in place, his eyes focused on me a bit more intently than usual.

Breaking eye contact and sitting on one of my new chairs, I exhaled in relief, my exhausted body appreciating the newfound comfort. The lasagne smelled great and I hoped it tasted good, too. I'd asked Ben to stay for dinner after he'd put together all the chairs – it turned out I was completely hopeless in that regard.

Ben took his first bite of the lasagne; I held my breath in anticipation, watching him chew. He hummed softly, nodding his head.

"This is really good," he said after he'd swallowed. "You're a natural."

He might have been teasing me again, or was being polite, but I didn't care. I grinned proudly, stupidly excited that he'd liked the food I'd made.

We ate and chatted for a while, the familiarity of the situation making me relax and let my guard down. Until I noticed Ben's eyes drifting to the clock on the wall more and more frequently. Unwillingly, my body tensed.

"Do you have somewhere to be?" I asked, irritation sneaking into my voice.

"Actually, yes," Ben said, pushing his empty plate away. "Thank you for dinner, Finn. If you need any help with anything else let me know."

I nodded, absentmindedly, watching him as he took his plate to the sink. I was wondering where he was hurrying off to this late. Well, it wasn't *that* late – only half six – but the thought that he might have a date tonight kept nagging at me, spiking my annoyance even higher.

Forcing myself to act normal, as if I couldn't care less where Ben was going, I saw him to the door and even waved at him as he climbed into his car. Leaning casually on the doorframe I folded my arms and watched him pull out of my driveway. His taillights disappeared round the corner, and as I was closing the door, movement across the street caught my eye. Rose was coming out of her house, the dog following behind her. A woman I supposed was her mother, although I've never seen her before, leaned out the window and called her name, but Rose didn't turn back. For a brief second she met my eyes across the road, but didn't wave or even smile. She kept walking away from the house, a strange sort of determination in her step, her hands balled into fists. Her mother shook her head and closed the window, drawing the curtains sharply.

The whole scene triggered me, anxiety fluttering in my belly. A need to protect Rose, to shield her from her mother, built inside me, and I nearly ran after her. Only... It wasn't any of my business, was it? Rose might not need protecting, her mother might not be a bad person. They could have just had an argument, or Rose was being the stubborn, often rude, teenager I'd grown to like.

The uneasy feeling remained, but I made myself close the door and go back inside. If Rose needed me I had no doubt she'd come to me, whether I liked it or not. For now it was better to mind my own business.

Back in the kitchen I cleaned the table and loaded the dishwasher, then put the leftover lasagne in the fridge. A red light was blinking on my phone, catching my attention. I swiped it from the counter, finding a text from Aiden.

What are you up to?

I snapped a photo of my new chairs and texted him back, sending him the photo with the caption:

Just built 6 chairs with my 2 bare hands.

TEN MILE BOTTOM

Not a second had passed before Aiden replied, sending me a whole row of laughing emojis.

Yeah, right. The Finney I know can't build a chair out of Lego let alone an actual chair that will hold a person's weight without collapsing.

I smirked and typed back.

*I *may* have had a little help from a sexy mechanic.*

My phone rang in my hand the moment I sent the text.
"What sexy mechanic?" Aiden said instead of a greeting.
I smiled widely. "Oh, you know, just someone I know."
Aiden laughed. "Is that so?"
"Mhm."
Aiden's voice had always served as a soothing balm on my bruised soul and today was no exception. Hearing his deep drawl, his quiet laughter, made all my flyaway parts come back together.

I sat in one of the chairs, propping my head on my hand as I told Aiden about everything that had happened in these past few days. It wasn't much – my life in Ten Mile Bottom was terribly boring – but he listened with interest, laughing softly or asking questions.

I told him about Ben. Or rather, about my obsession with the guy. I couldn't judge Aiden's reaction without seeing his face – his bright hazel eyes could never lie to me, even if he tried to keep his expression blank. His voice seemed a bit reserved as he asked about Ben, though. I tried hard not to grow defensive, fully aware that hooking up with someone when I was trying to focus on myself was not a good idea. I didn't need Aiden to tell me that.

The thing was, hooking up with Ben wasn't my priority. The guy was hot and I was intensely attracted to him, but the thought of a one-night stand with him, then never talking to him again, never eating homemade food or hearing his laugh, made me nauseous.

I cleared my throat, realising I'd spaced out, stretching the pause in the conversation for too long. Needing to change the subject, I asked,

"Aren't you sick of the idyllic Irish countryside yet?"

Aiden sighed heavily, then took a moment to answer. "I think I am."

"Yeah? Going back to London?" As much as I wanted to I couldn't curtail the envy weaving its way into my heart. I craved London and my old life as much as I still craved the bliss of drugs, and Aiden going back without me felt like the ultimate betrayal.

"I don't know."

I knew what the guarded uncertainty in his voice meant. Just like me, Aiden craved to go back but was afraid of falling back on old, comfortable habits, disappointing and hurting the people he loved.

"Mum wants me to stay. Permanently," he said, his voice pained. "I love her, you know I do, but honestly – I can't stay here forever. Even if I find my own place. I just can't, Finn. I'm climbing the walls as it is."

I hummed, letting him know I was listening while he got everything out.

"You know how she is, and it's only gotten worse ever since the... incident."

"Heart attack," I corrected him. He wasn't going to downplay what had happened, ever. I was going to carry that burden for the rest of my life and I wasn't going to allow Aiden to let me forget.

"Heart attack," he said softly. He took a deep breath, as if buying himself some time to decide what to say next. "She's become so overprotective, always watching me as if I'm about to break. I can't handle it anymore. I feel like I'm suffocating."

I hummed again, drawing circles on the table with the tip of my finger. I loved Aiden's mum. Yes, she was a bit overprotective and had a tendency to meddle in his life, but there was never any agenda behind her actions. Fiana was painfully honest and her actions always transparent, and always wrapped in so much love for Aiden. I'd often been jealous of their close relationship, but Fiana made me feel as part of the family, treating me as a brother to Aiden and often smothering me with the same love.

"Plus, she's been force feeding me and I must have gained a hundred pounds. None of my clothes fit anymore."

"Last time I saw you, you were dangerously underweight, Aiden. If you've gained a few pounds that's a good thing."

I could hear his eyeroll through the phone as he said, "Look who's talking."

"Actually, I've started running every morning, and all the hard work I'm doing on the house has made me bulk up."

I'd jogged once. I wanted to turn it into a habit, but I was too lazy.

Aiden laughed heartily for two solid minutes.

"Alright, settle down, dickhead," I said, offended that he hadn't believed my lies. "I'll send you a torso pic in a minute."

He laughed even harder.

CHAPTER TWELVE

I'd never been a morning person. But for some inexplicable reason I often woke up at the crack of dawn ever since I'd moved to the country.

Must be the clean fucking air.

This morning, when I found myself wide awake at 7 AM, the bright June sun already trying to sneak through the curtains, I briefly contemplated going for a jog. Who was I kidding, though? Unless someone forcibly dragged me out of bed and kicked me out of the house, no sort of morning exercise was happening any time soon. The air wasn't clean enough to brainwash me to such extent.

Stubbornly, I tossed and turned for a little while longer until I got annoyed with myself for not falling back asleep, and got up. The notebook I'd made a habit of taking everywhere with me was sitting on the night stand, my hands itching to take it.

Might as well.

After a quick trip to the bathroom, I grabbed the notebook and settled in the reading nook I'd made for myself in the alcove of the bedroom's bay window. One of the voices in my head was louder than all the others this morning. Until now I'd mainly scribbled notes and ideas, a few lines here and there, a couple of character bios I'd wanted to play with later, but today the new voice didn't let me do anything else but write about him.

TEN MILE BOTTOM

By the time I'd finished jotting down his thoughts and feelings, some scenes that kept pestering me and bits of dialogue I couldn't get out of my head, it was nearly lunch time. My stomach growled, jolting me back to reality. I was a little nauseous because of my empty stomach, but I couldn't help but grin. I felt lighter than I had in a long time, remembering how much I loved the feeling of getting so absorbed in a fictional world that I forgot what the real world around me looked like.

I was about to hop down from the alcove and head to the kitchen for much needed food and coffee when I saw Ruby – Steve's wife – coming out of her house, carrying what looked like a plate in her hands. I'd seen her a few times in her front garden, tending to her flowers or talking animatedly to the mailman, and she'd smiled and waved at me, but we'd never actually talked. I should have probably gone to introduce myself but I never did. Mainly because I was a grumpy Londoner who wasn't here to make friends.

Even though people kept butting into my life, forcing me to like them.

I watched as she crossed the road separating our houses and headed straight to my door. As she neared, I could clearly see the dish she was carrying contained some sort of pie. My traitorous mouth watered, my stomach growling again in show of support.

Dammit. I really wanted that pie, which I could bet she'd baked herself and was probably still nice and warm. But I didn't want to talk to anyone right now. Etiquette probably dictated that I should invite her in, offer her tea or coffee, cut the pie and sit down together for a chat.

It was the last thing I wanted to do. I had to pretend to be nice, and I really wasn't up to it. But I couldn't be rude to her, could I? If it'd been Rose trekking to my door I'd have told her to piss off and gone back inside without a second thought. She would have probably ignored me and come in anyway, but that wasn't the point. I couldn't be rude to a nice, old lady bringing me pie.

The doorbell rang, and my stomach fluttered uncomfortably. I could always pretend I wasn't home, but I wanted the damn pie.

So I went and opened the door, leaning on the frame in case she got any ideas I'd invite her in. I wasn't that desperate for the pie. Besides, I could be nice to her at the door, right? Pretend I was super busy or going out, or something.

"Hi," I said, plastering my most charming smile on my face. "You must be Ruby."

"I am," Ruby said, her dark eyes crinkling at the corners as she smiled. "Glad to finally meet you, Finn. Steve's told me all about you."

I wondered how could Steve have told her "all about me" when we'd talked once, but I let it slide. The pie smelled heavenly, and of course my stomach growled with renewed energy, demanding the food it sensed was close by.

Ruby's smile widened. "I made this cherry pie this morning for you, I hope you like it." She handed me the dish, her shrewd gaze never leaving my face. Ruby was no more than five-foot-two, but the determination in her eyes left little doubt she could make a grown man cry when she wanted to.

"Thank you, that's so nice of you," I said, taking the pie, and grinning wider, hoping to charm her into liking me, and possibly bringing more pie in the future. "Unfortunately, I have an appointment in town in about half an hour and I've got to rush out in about five minutes." My face fell as if not being able to invite her in and share the pie over a cup of tea and local gossip was the worst thing imaginable.

Ruby waved a hand. "Don't worry, dear. I have a Pilates class in twenty minutes. I just wanted to properly introduce myself."

I gaped at her. She must have been in her late sixties, and yet her life was more exciting than mine. I remembered Steve mentioning a book club Ruby frequented, and judging by her impeccable blonde bob, subtle make-up and fashionable clothes, she was taking good care of herself. How people found motivation to do any of that at her age was beyond me. I was twenty four and most days I couldn't be bothered to shave or comb my hair, let alone go to Pilates classes and book clubs and whatnot.

"No worries," I said, closing my gaping mouth and morphing my lips into a smile again. "Maybe some other time." *Fucking idiot, why did I say that?* I hope she didn't take it as an invitation. "Thanks for the pie," I called after her as she walked down my driveway.

Safely inside my house again, I exhaled in relief. That exchange had taken more out of me than I was willing to give.

But at least I'd gotten a freshly baked pie out of it.

I paced around the living room, glaring at the open laptop on the coffee table. I'd spent nearly the entire day writing in my notebook until I thought I was ready to transcribe all I'd written into a more legible format. And maybe even start transforming it into a linear story that made sense.

My mental block at seeing the blank page of the Word document had prevented me from writing a single syllable.

And now, as I paced, frustrated with myself, I tried to find a solution to this mess. I wanted to sit down and write this story. I hadn't felt the urge in a long time and I wanted to do something about it before my apathy clouded my brain again. And yet, looking at the blank page made my heart rate pick up and my palms sweat.

Thankfully, the doorbell saved me from any more agonising.

"Hey, Finn," Rose said when I opened the door, something in her voice and posture giving me a pause. She was holding Eren, a book bag slung over her shoulder, and giving off a weird vibe, her usual confident demeanour gone.

"Hi, Rose, what's up?" My eyes slid over her shoulder to her house, noticing the unusual amount of cars parked in and around the driveway. Rose followed my gaze, turning to look over her shoulder, but she didn't comment.

"Can I stay here for a while? I have homework to do and it's a bit noisy in my house."

Her dog leaned towards me in Rose's arms, sniffing at me, her tongue hanging from her mouth. I pet her on the head and scratched under her chin before stepping aside and letting them in.

Rose thanked me but didn't volunteer any more information, so I kept my mouth shut. Besides, I could use some company to distract me from angsting over my writing. Or the lack of.

"Why are you even studying? Isn't it summer holidays?" I asked as we settled into the living room. Unknowingly, Rose took my spot on the sofa, tucking her legs under her and spreading books everywhere. Eren decided to snuggle next to me in the armchair and promptly fall asleep.

"I'm starting my last year in Sixth Form in September and want to get the best possible score on my A levels." She opened a thick book and placed it next to her, holding it open with the help of two other books. Then she fished a laptop from her bag, placing it on her lap and turning it on. "What's your Wi-Fi password?"

I told her the password, then asked,

"What A levels are you taking?"

"Maths, English, Psychology, History, and Media Studies."

I arched an eyebrow at her.

"There's this scholarship I want to get," Rose said, talking as she typed on the keyboard. I never understood how people could do that; I could barely focus on one thing at a time. "Worst case scenario I'll get a student loan because there's no way in hell I'm staying here after Sixth Form, but I really don't want it to come to that."

"You don't get along with your mum?" I asked tentatively.

"Something like that." I felt her clam up, her whole body on the defensive now.

I didn't pry anymore. She'd tell me if she wanted to.

With the damn dog snoring next to me, and Rose working quietly on her laptop, I had no choice but to pull my own computer on my lap. Eren lifted her chin as I moved and jostled her, then promptly placed it on my thigh, looking up at me as if asking for permission. I balanced the laptop on my other thigh and raised an eyebrow at her. Content, she closed her eyes again.

For some reason opening the blank document didn't look so menacing anymore. I placed my notebook on the armrest and started writing.

When the door bell rang both Eren and I startled. It took me a second to drag my mind out of the story and back to reality as I looked around the room, dazed.

"I'll get it," Rose said, already standing up.

"Thanks."

She waved me off and hurried to open the door. I heard a male voice, but couldn't quite understand what was being said. The exchange was short, though, and soon Rose trudged back to the living room carrying a box. She set it on the table with a grunt.

"What the fuck is that?" I asked, eyeing the box suspiciously.

"I've no idea, but it's heavy as shit." She flopped back down on the sofa.

Eren jumped from the armchair and went to sniff around the box.

"There's two more by the door. Bigger ones," Rose said casually as she started typing again.

Curiosity piqued, I stood and approached the box, pulling at the tape holding it closed. I'd had my mail redirected from my flat in London so the box was covered with address labels stuck on top of address labels. It was also pretty beat up, so my guess was it took a while to find me.

"That'll be much easier if you get a knife," Rose mumbled, not looking away from the screen.

Admittedly, it did take a while to peel the tape off but I couldn't be bothered to go to the kitchen and get a knife. I'd dedicated too much time to this to give up now. Seeing as I ignored her comment, Rose shook her head and came to stand next to me. Not helping, mind you, just critically staring at my attempt to open the huge box.

I pulled the last of the tape with flourish and lifted the lid, only to be faced with paperback copies of my first book, *Lost Silence*. There must have been at least fifty of them.

"What's that?" Rose asked, peering at the contents of the box and picking up a book. "Why do you need so many copies of *Lost Silence*? My friend Andrè loves this book, by the way. He has every edition ever released."

She looked up at me and frowned at my dumbfounded expression. I'd been racking my brain for an excuse to have this many copies of the same book, and I got nothing. Rose studied me, then looked back at the book, realisation hitting her as she looked at me with wide eyes.

"Oh. My. God!" She exclaimed, sticking the book in my face. "You're Finnegan J. Rowe?" It wasn't really a question, more like an accusation.

I pushed her hand holding the book away. "You can't tell anyone, Rose." I said, running a hand through my hair. "People are already up in my business way more than I'd have liked."

Rose put the book back in the box and sat back down. Sensing an available lap, Eren jumped up on the sofa and lay across Rose's legs.

"Of course I'm not going to tell anyone, Finn." She bit her lip and gave me the biggest puppy eyes I'd ever seen.

"What?"

"Can I please just tell my friend Andrè?"

"No."

I walked out of the living room to check on the other boxes. She'd been right, they were fucking huge. There was no way I'd be able to drag them inside without pulling a muscle on my back. "Come help me with these boxes," I called back to her.

"Only if I can tell Andrè!"

"Rose!"

She appeared in the doorway, folding her arms.

"Andrè's not going to tell anyone else, I promise." I ignored her, hands on my hips, contemplating how to move the fucking things. She came closer. "Finn, listen to me." When I faced her, I fully intended to tell her to stop nagging me but the vulnerability in her eyes stopped me. "Andrè and I don't have anyone to tell. We... don't have many other friends." Her arms flapped at her sides helplessly. "So you don't have to worry about that. Besides, Andrè is solid, I trust him implicitly."

I still wasn't convinced. They may not have many other friends but that didn't stop them from blabbing on social media or to get attention in school.

As soon as the thought crossed my mind I knew it was the self-preservation talking. I didn't know that Andrè guy but I trusted Rose, for some weird reason.

"Look," she said, coming closer. "Andrè's gay and he had a hard time coming to terms with it when we were younger. And then he found your book and it helped him deal with everything, and then eventually come out. He must have read it a hundred times, obsessing over it every time. I promise you he won't say anything if I ask him not to. He idolises you, Finn, he'll never do anything to hurt you."

"Just grab the other end of the box, will you?" I said with a resigned sigh. Rose grinned, then came round to help with the boxes.

We moved them eventually, both of us grunting, and I nearly lost a toe when Rose dropped her end, narrowly missing my bare foot. But we managed, and as I stood there, glaring at the huge boxes in the middle of my living room, I realised I had a very unpleasant conversation coming with my agent.

I didn't know why she hadn't dropped me yet. Probably some sort of sense of loyalty. Angie had been with me from the beginning, both of us young and stupid, but wildly ambitious. She'd believed in my book even when I hadn't, and that faith in me and my work had scored her a place in one of the biggest literary agencies in London, and a lucrative three book contract for me.

"I have to give my agent a call," I said to Rose who had sat back on the sofa, Eren in her lap. "It'll probably take a while."

"It's fine," Rose said with a shrug, gently removing Eren from her lap and pulling her laptop closer. She didn't insist on telling that friend of hers again, and at least for now we seemed to have struck a truce.

I found my flip-flops by the back door and slipped them on, opening the French windows and stepping outside. The mild evening air felt good on my skin as I sat in my favourite lounge chair and put my feet up on another one. The sun had nearly set behind the trees, a wayward orange sunbeam still visible behind the branches, but not for long. I couldn't hear any other sound but birds chirping nearby and the occasional car driving by my house. It was peaceful, and probably for the first time since I'd arrived I managed to take a deep breath, exhale, and not feel trapped. I could even say I was starting to like it here.

With a shake of my head to get rid of these unwelcome thoughts, I pulled out my phone from my pocket and thumbed through the contacts until I found Angie's number.

She picked up on the second ring.

"Well, well," she drawled and I couldn't help but smile. I'd missed her voice. "It's alive! It can make calls!"

I chuckled. "Hey, Angie."

"And it talks! Would you look at that?"

"Alright, enough drama," I said without any heat in my voice. Angie was entitled to all the drama she wanted. I had ignored her calls for months.

"Finn, you bastard!" She started, but then paused uncertainly. "Wait, are you alright?"

"I'm fine."

"You dickhead! Where the hell have you been?"

"It's a long story."

"I always have time for my favourite client."

I laughed, clutching the phone harder, my heart rate already picking up as I made up my mind to tell her everything. I hadn't talked to her since before Dad died, and it wasn't fair. We were friends before anything else, and she'd stood by me ever since I was a wide-eyed college kid with big dreams and nothing much else.

"I'm sorry, Angie," I began, and then told her everything.

The light was on in the living room when I returned. And Rose was still there. She pretended to be engrossed in whatever she was doing on her laptop but I could feel she was vibrating with need to know why I'd been on the phone for nearly an hour.

"Don't you need to go home?" I asked, sitting down in the armchair. Eren immediately appeared out of nowhere and jumped on me.

Rose shrugged. "Not really."

"You can't stay here forever."

"Why not?"

I threw her a look that made her roll her eyes, but she bit her lip nervously before she spoke.

"Mum's having people over and I don't really want to be there." She shrugged as if it wasn't a big deal. I knew that shrug all too well, and I knew it *was* a big deal, but there wasn't much you could do, so shrugging is all you had left.

"What do you need all the books for?" Rose asked, her change of subject anything but smooth. I let her have it.

"Angie – my agent – wants me to sign them for this charity event she's organising."

It was actually a pretty cool idea, an auction for signed books and all sorts of author swag to benefit a charity for children with dyslexia. Angie'd begged me to go to the event, but right now I couldn't imagine anything worse than having to schmooze with people I didn't even know.

Actually, Ben running out on me last night, and not texting at all today was worse.

"That's cool," she said, casting me a sly look. "Can I bring Andrè over tomorrow?"

Honestly, I didn't have the energy to argue anymore.

"Whatever. The whole damn town probably knows anyway."

"You said you didn't tell anyone."

"I didn't. But Ben recognised me, and I'm pretty sure Ruby and Steve know, too. Why would she bring me pie otherwise?"

Rose looked confused for a moment as if my words weren't making much sense. "To be nice?" She said as if I was the biggest idiot she'd met. "You're not used to people being nice to you, are you, Finn?"

"Not without a reason."

I'd never had an eighteen-year-old girl look at me with pity in her big blue eyes, but when Rose did, I wanted to disappear rather than deal with her sympathy.

She opened her mouth to say something, but changed her mind. Eren moved in my lap and I petted her head without taking much notice. She settled again with a big yawn. I'd have given anything to be as spoiled and unconcerned with the world as Eren.

"Ben recognised you?" Rose asked with a cheeky smile.

So we were still talking about this.

"Yes. And we had a moment. And then a date? I don't know anymore." I ran a hand through my hair and slid even further down in the armchair. "But he ran out on me last night, saying he had somewhere to be, and hasn't texted or called today, and I don't know what to think. I also don't want to look like I'm desperate and be the one to call him all the time."

Rose didn't say anything so I turned to look at her. She was watching me with a smile and I had no idea what had caused the excitement on her face. But I had to admit, it felt good to talk to someone about these things. Even if it was a teenage girl who was strangely attached to me and wouldn't leave my house.

"Look, I don't know Ben well, but he doesn't seem like the type to play games and string you along. Are you sure you didn't do something to push him away?"

"I'm sure," I said without much conviction, my overactive brain already replaying every moment we'd been together and everything I'd said.

Rose raised an eyebrow, doubtful. "Even if that's true," she said in a tone that obviously humoured me and she didn't believe for a second it was true. "There must be a reason, Finn." Her eyes glazed over for a while as if she was thinking. I let her do it, closing my eyes and petting the damn dog. The small gesture and the feel of silky fur under my fingers settled something inside me I couldn't fight anymore. "What happened when he told you he knew who you are?"

"Why?"

"Because if you reacted as hotly as when I figured it out, I bet he was embarrassed and maybe wanted to put some space between you. Not come out as a creepy stalker."

I hated to admit that actually made sense. And that I hadn't thought of it myself. So I kept my cool and shrugged.

"Maybe, who knows," I said with finality. For once Rose took the hint and let me be.

CHAPTER THIRTEEN

The next day I woke up with the decision to text Ben already made. I didn't want to give my brain any time to come up with some irrelevant excuse so I got my phone from the nightstand and opened the text message app.

My fingers hovered over the keyboard for a while, uncertainty already creeping in. No, I was doing it. If I let whatever we had fizzle away just because I was too stubborn and too proud to actually go for it I'd be even a bigger loser than if he brushed me off.

Decision made once again, I typed.

Hey, what are you doing tonight? Wanna hang out?

I read the two simple sentences a hundred times. I added a winky face. Deleted it. Added an 'x'. Deleted it. In the end settled for a smiley face and, closing my eyes, clicked send.

My heart started beating faster while I stared at the phone, waiting for an immediate reply. Soon I realised it wasn't coming. So, instead of driving myself into a frenzy, I used the upsurge of energy to hop in the shower.

I took my time washing my hair, shaving, putting moisturiser and brushing my teeth twice as long as the usual time, all the while thinking about Ben's reply. Thankfully, when I got out of the bathroom, my eyes darting in the direction of the phone on my bed, the little red light was blinking. A grin crept on my face and I didn't even try to stop it. Even the fleeting thought that the notification could be for anything else couldn't wipe the smile off my face.

I fell on the bed, still a bit wet from the shower but I didn't care, and reached for my phone. Seeing Ben's text made my already huge grin grow impossibly wider.

Hey, I have something to do, but you can come with me if you want. It'll be fun.

Not caring if I looked too eager, I replied straight away.

What is it?

Surprisingly, Ben's text came right away as well. I wanted to imagine him sitting in the garage on his break, staring at his phone and grinning like I was. I didn't even care if it wasn't true, I'd already conjured the image in my head.

You'll see.

He wasn't going to tell? But how was I supposed to dress? What if it was some sort of a networking event and I was wearing jeans? Or he was meeting with friends in a pub?

My head was starting to spin with all the unpleasant possibilities I'd managed to come up with in the space of a few seconds.

You're not gonna tell me?

Nope.

Anything I should know beforehand?

Nope.

God, I didn't like this. My anxiety piqued, but then I remembered Ben's kind smile, his calming presence and those gorgeous, green eyes, and I knew he wouldn't do something to make me uncomfortable or put me on the spot. There was no logical reason to feel this way – Ben didn't even know me well enough to know what would make me uncomfortable. Did he?
I typed my reply before I could change my mind.

OK.

I'll pick you up at half five?

Sure.

For the first time in two years I opened my laptop and ignored the anxiety of seeing the blank document, letting the words inside me pour out on the page freely, not thinking of the style or grammar or even fucking spelling. I just wrote.

Ben came at exactly half five. I heard the rumble of his car's engine outside before he'd even rang the bell. Not that I was listening for it or anything.
"Is this OK?" I asked when I opened the door, gesturing to my outfit. I'd decided on simple and casual – a pair of jeans, a soft

t-shirt I absolutely loved, and a pair of Converse instead of flip-flips.

"Yeah," he said, his gaze sliding over my body like a caress. "You look great, Finn."

"You too." I willed my body not to react but I was sure a slight blush must have crept on my cheeks.

Ben's smile made me forget all my worries, though. He was looking at me as if he saw something in me that nobody else did, and he wanted it all for himself.

Grabbing my keys, I locked the door behind me and followed Ben to his car.

"You're not gonna tell me where we're going?" I asked once inside. "I *really* don't like surprises."

Ben must have sensed something in my voice because he glanced at me with a slight frown, and then said,

"I volunteer at a youth centre in Cambridge a few times a month. I had a class last week with the kids interested in mechanics and we built this super cool remote control car." He grinned and glanced at me again. I could imagine Ben working with the kids, his youthful appearance and enthusiasm making him seem like one of them, his knowledge the only thing setting him apart.

Something clicked in my brain right then and I asked, "Is that where you went the other night?"

"Yes." He smiled at me as if he knew exactly what I'd though back then. Relief that he hadn't been on a date after all washed over me, and I returned his smile, feeling my cheeks burn hot.

"That sounds like fun," I said, looking away. I didn't particularly like kids, but spending the evening with Ben in his element was something I could definitely do.

Shaking his head a little Ben said, "It's not what we're doing tonight. The mechanics class is twice a month, but I also do another one every week."

"Oh?"

We got in the car, slamming the doors behind us in unison. Ben started the engine and adjusted the air-conditioning, but turned in his seat to look at me instead of putting the car in gear.

"Yeah. Maggie, she runs the centre, made me do it because their regular instructor went on maternity leave. They needed someone to fill in until they could find a permanent replacement."

"So..." I said, uncertainly. "What is it?"

Ben's smile grew positively wicked as he said, "Salsa dancing."

Conflicting emotions erupted inside me, making me hot all over. On one hand, watching Ben dance would be a dream come true; on the other I hadn't done any sort of dancing, apart from swaying in a crowded club, high and drunk, in... ever. The thought of having to take part in the lesson sent hot shivers down my spine. I squirmed in the seat.

Sensing my discomfort, Ben quickly said, "You won't have to dance, Finn. Don't worry." Something eased inside me and I visibly slumped in the seat. "The kids are great and we usually have a ton of fun, you can just grab a cup of coffee and watch. We should be done by eight and we can go get a bite to eat if you want."

"I'd like that," I said, quietly, Ben's reassurance like a caress to my anxious soul.

The kids swarmed Ben the moment he walked in. I'd been right, he did look like one of them with his jeans and t-shirt, wild hair, and sparkling green eyes. But what made him seem even younger was his charming smile, so wide and contagious and genuine that I felt like a fraud.

As we walked in and Ben got taken by the kids, all asking questions and teasing him, I hung back, not wanting to intrude. The hall the lesson was held in wasn't huge, but it was big enough for about twenty kids to move around easily. There were mirrors lining two of the walls and chairs tucked away in a corner. I pulled one out and sat, clutching my takeaway coffee cup.

I watched Ben in his element, talking to the kids and to the two adults on the other side of the hall, and even though I liked being left alone, I kinda felt left out. But before I could start feeling sorry for myself yet again, Ben turned around, his eyes scanning the hall until they landed on me.

"Finn!" He called, waving me over. I was both relieved and nervous as I stood up and walked over to him.

Every single pair of eyes was staring at me. It was a miracle I didn't trip as I sauntered over to Ben.

"Guys, this is Finn," he said, wrapping an arm around my shoulders as I reached him. "He's a friend of mine, so be nice." His mock stern tone as he aimed a glare, or what he thought was a glare, at the kids was quite amusing. I bit my lip against a smile.

Apparently, I wasn't interesting enough to hold the kids' attention for long. After saying, "Hi, Finn" as Ben instructed, they all continued talking over each other and giggling as they started their warm up.

"Bring the chair over here," Ben said, leaning closer to me and pointing to the near wall. "I don't like you sitting there, all by yourself in the corner."

"Nobody puts Baby in the corner, right?"

A deep, throaty laugh burst from Ben and his eyes twinkled with amusement as he held my gaze.

"Right."

I went to get my chair and as I turned around to drag it to the other side of the hall, one of the men was holding a guitar that had seemingly materialised out of nowhere, and was adjusting a stool to sit on. The other was sitting in front of a pair of bongos, his smile wide as he talked to Ben.

"Alright, everyone, line up," Ben said, clapping his hands to get the kids' attention.

With practiced precision, they spread through the width of the hall, leaving enough space between them to move freely.

"Give me a beat, Marcus," Ben said, turning to Marcus with a wink. The guy grinned and started playing the bongos in a steady rhythm, the guitar smoothly joining him with a sensual melody.

I sipped my coffee and watched as the kids launched into a practiced routine, moving easily to the rhythm, Ben standing in front, counting and giving them directions they didn't really need. When the warm-up routine was over, everyone paired up, and that was when the fun began. I wished I was as carefree as these kids, letting go and dancing, not once looking in the mirrors to check my posture.

Ben walked among them, correcting their steps if needed, fixing their stance and encouraging them, all the while smiling and humming to the songs the musicians played. I recognised some of the melodies as popular songs I'd heard on the radio, with a tiny twist in the beat to fit the salsa rhythm.

Time flew as I observed the lesson, my leg bouncing with the music, and my face sore from smiling so much. Ben was joking with the kids, making them relax and feel comfortable while at the same time showing them the proper steps until he was satisfied they got it. As I watched him, something warm and heavy grew in my chest, making it harder to breathe.

I was falling for a guy I hadn't even kissed yet.

The realisation blindsided me, my breath catching. It wasn't possible, was it?

The edges of a panic attack appeared in my vision, my breathing becoming more and more laboured.

"Finn," I heard Ben say before I saw him standing next to me. "You OK? You look a little pale."

It was irrational and didn't make any sense, but his presence and his voice calmed me. I didn't know why. Nobody had been able to ward off a panic attack before, not even Aiden, but as Ben put a hand on my shoulder I felt the panic leech from the spot where he'd touched me.

"I'm fine," I managed to say and even smile a little. He didn't seem convinced but let me be.

"You sure you don't want to give it a go?" He inclined his head towards the dancing kids. "I could use a partner to show them the next move."

I couldn't say no to that smile.

Ben was as surprised as I was when I nodded and stood up, letting him lead the way to the front of the class. Nobody made any comment about my sudden urge to dance, their eyes glued on Ben as he spoke.

"Right. Finn's agreed to help me out here to show you guys this next move."

Wrapping his arms around me, Ben led the way in a simple move that, magically, I managed to get straight away. With a small gesture of his hand behind my back, Ben gave a signal to the musicians and they started playing again. The kids around us started dancing, too, imitating whatever we were doing. How I even managed to move the way Ben wanted me to, I had no idea. What was even weirder was that I didn't feel self-conscious at all. I wasn't even thinking about the steps. Like an idiot, I stared at Ben, delighted I was finally so close I could see the little freckles on his nose and the gold specks in his green eyes, and let him lead my body into the salsa. When he smiled at me, I felt I could do anything.

All too soon, Ben let go of me and turned to the kids, announcing it was nearly the end of the lesson and it was time for the cool down. They all sat on the floor and started stretching while the musicians put their instruments away in a cupboard built in the wall.

"That was great, thank you," I said to Ben. He touched my forearm and nodded, then stepped aside to help Marcus put the bongos away.

Not having much to do, I felt stupid just standing there staring lustfully after him, so I brought my chair back to the pile on the other side and decided to go find the toilets. When I returned, the hall was empty and Ben was turning off the lights when he saw me.

"Hey, I was wondering where you went." He came closer, too close, our shoes nearly touching. "I thought you may have run away on me."

Like that's a real possibility.

I scoffed and the bastard smirked, reaching to entwine our fingers together. My heart beat so fast I thought I'd combust. Ben's gaze slid to my lips and stayed there for a long moment. I was certain he'd kiss me, so certain that I licked my lips in anticipation. The gesture had the opposite effect on him.

"Let's go grab something to eat. I'm starving," Ben said, breaking the moment.

I couldn't help the disappointment that washed over me like a bucket of ice water. Ben squeezed my fingers, reminding me he still held my hand. He didn't let go as he led me out of the hall and to his car, and just like that my body was warm all over again.

Cambridge town centre was quaint and buzzing with life. People milled around, groups of teenagers chatting and laughing, families with children running around, and elderly couples holding hands. It was past eight o'clock but there were still some stalls open in the market, so we grabbed some pastries, grilled German sausages, freshly baked breads, and fruit juices and headed for the park. I took out my phone and snapped a photo as we passed by one of the colleges. The old building stood proud in the midst of town, its lawns cut to perfection, its old facade clean and well-maintained. Every building had its charm, whether it was old or recently built, the small antique shops and cafes huddled inside them the only reminder of the time period we lived in.

As we walked, Ben pointed out some of the more interesting sights, like King's College and Trinity College, Pembroke, and the thirteenth century building of Peterhouse, and I took pictures of everything. When we reached an alcove between two residential buildings, Ben took my hand and pulled me through it, leading us to a courtyard between the buildings. There was a fountain in the middle of the yard with a stone statue of a mermaid on top of it. A vintage red bicycle was parked behind it, and pots with blooming flowers hung from the first floor balcony over it. The whole scene was like a postcard. When I took out my phone to take a couple of photos, Ben pulled me closer and we took a selfie in front of the running fountain, with the bicycle and the flowers in the background. We were both grinning like teenagers on a first date. My heart skipped a beat as I studied the photo, and felt Ben's hand on the small of my back. He peered at the screen and said,

"We look cute."

Our shoulders were touching, his hand was on my back, the heat from his palm seeping through the thin t-shirt I wore. I couldn't breathe. My hands shook as I turned the screen off and put the phone in my pocket. Ben didn't move away. He turned his head, his nose touching my cheek, and he nuzzled my skin ever so slightly.

"Finn," he murmured against my cheek, his breath tickling my skin. "I really want to kiss you."

Turning my head to look into his eyes, our lips nearly touched.

"What's stopping you?" I asked.

He didn't answer right away, a sexy little frown appearing between his brows.

"I don't want you to think I'm doing it because you're Finnegan J Rowe," he finally said.

At some point, I'd forgotten who I was when I was with Ben. The fact that he'd read my work and claimed to love it was tucked away at the back of my mind, nearly forgotten. When I was with him, I was me. Just *me*. Not some famous author or a recovering addict or a wayward son and brother. Somehow, Ben lifted all the weight off my shoulders and let me be myself without any prejudice.

"Why are you doing it then?" I asked with a smirk.

Ben's frown eased, a playful twinkle dancing in his eyes.

"Because you're sexy," he said, placing the bag with the food on the ground, and moving his hand to the side of my neck. "And cute. And every time you laugh I want to pull you close." He did pull me closer, his hand on my back more insistent, pressing my body to his.

Leaning in ever so slightly, Ben pressed his lips to the corner of my mouth. The feathery touch burned my skin and I closed my eyes, my lips parting with a soft exhale. Ben's thumb stroked my cheek, and I felt both overwhelmed and wanting more. When his lips left my skin it was me who chased his mouth, pressing it to his tentatively. Ben's lips parted, welcoming me in, his hands clutched at the t-shirt on my back, pulling me in even closer until our bodies were fully pressed together. I weaved my hands around his neck, burying my fingers in his hair.

Ben moaned as our kiss turned more frantic, clutching at each other as if afraid the other would disappear. I'd never been kissed so thoroughly, so sweetly yet dirty at the same time. Ben bit my lips, sucked on my tongue, devoured my mouth as if it was his for the taking.

Someone wolf whistled, the sound jerking us out of the lust filled bubble we'd created. The world started taking shape around me again and I saw a guy wearing only a pair of shorts smoking on a balcony on the second floor. He watched us in a way that made me uncomfortable, so I picked up the bag, grabbed Ben's hand and pulled him towards the alcove.

"Let's go find a nice, secluded spot in the park, shall we? I'm starving."

Ben smirked and followed me without complaint.

Walking in the park with one of the locals had its advantages. Ben expertly led the way to a secluded spot, a small garden of sorts with flowers blooming everywhere, a cobblestone path leading to the canal nearby, and a single bench hidden beneath an oak tree. We sat, opening the bag eagerly to take out all the food and drinks we'd bought. I was starving, and judging by Ben's enthusiasm, he was too.

The food had gone cold, but neither of us seemed to care. We ate with our hands, sharing the different sausages and breads, and feeding each other sweet pastries. I was lightheaded with happiness. The sound of Ben's voice as he talked both relaxed me and sent shivers of pleasure down my body. After the kiss something had shifted, and Ben wasn't afraid to touch me anymore. He angled his body so that he was always facing me, his fingers finding their way to entwine with mine, or lightly caressing my skin, or resting on my thigh. If I'd known he'd become so affectionate and tactile I'd have kissed him a long time ago.

"I think I like this version of you better," I said with a smile as we put the leftovers and rubbish away, then slid closer to each other. Ben casually draped his arm over my shoulders, nuzzling my temple, placing a soft kiss on the same spot.

"What do you mean?"

"Well, before, you jumped back every time we were close to each other, and wouldn't touch me unless you absolutely had to. In all honesty I had my doubts you liked me at all, but then you'd invite me to hang out and cook for me, or come round to mine and be all charming and flirty. My head was spinning from all the different signals you were giving me."

I turned slightly to look at him and judge his reaction. I'd kept my voice light, not wanting to sound as if I was accusing him, but I still wanted to find out what had been going through his head before today.

Ben's face grew serious and his green eyes darkened. "I told you before, in the courtyard," he said, his thumb coming to stroke my cheekbone. "After the way you clammed up when I told you I knew who you were and that I was a fan, I didn't want you to think I was cosying up to you because of that." He placed a soft kiss in the corner of my mouth, and I had to admit – I was starting to like that. "I wanted to get to know you, the real you, not the person from social media, and I wanted to give you a chance to get to know me, and see I wasn't after you like some obsessed fan." He paused, his eyes searching mine, as if debating whether to say whatever else was on his mind.

"What is it?" I asked.

"I don't know if that's a good thing, but..." He bit his lip, lowering his lashes to my lips. "I don't think of you as Finnegan J Rowe anymore. That person who'd post pictures of himself in a nightclub, his cheeks decorated in glitter, or at a glitzy party with other celebrities, or jetting off on an exotic holiday in the middle of winter... That person seems like someone else."

"It's a good thing," I said quietly, palming his neck and pulling him closer. I kissed him slowly, exploring his mouth, tasting the sweet juice we'd drank. He matched my pace, sliding his tongue over mine, sucking gently on my lips, swallowing the little noises of pleasure and arousal I made.

The truth was, I needed the distraction so that it dulled the guilt I'd started to feel at Ben's words. It was the perfect opportunity to tell him why I wasn't that self-obsessed party boy anymore. Why I'd moved in the middle of fucking nowhere. Why the Finnegan J Rowe he spoke of was dead.

But I couldn't.

I couldn't risk Ben rejecting me because of my mistakes. Not when I was starting to feel happy for the first time in ages. It was selfish, I knew that, but tonight I wanted us to remain in this little bubble we'd created, kiss and laugh and hold hands, and not be plagued by the past.

I'd tell him tomorrow.

CHAPTER FOURTEEN

A text alert beeped close to my head. I reached blindly for the phone I'd dropped somewhere on the bed last night. When I couldn't find it, I cracked a tired eye, cursing the bright sunshine streaming through the windows, and then myself for forgetting to close the curtains last night.

In my defence, I'd gotten home in the early hours of the morning, exhausted but drunk on happiness. Drunk on Ben. We'd walked around Cambridge until well past midnight, holding hands and talking, ducking into the shadows for a few kisses so intense they'd made my insides melt with pleasure.

A little shiver ran through me as I remembered Ben's mouth on mine. My cock, already sporting morning wood, took notice of my thoughts and pulsed with need to be touched. I snuck my hand under the covers, giving it a squeeze and a few leisurely strokes, closing my eyes as I remembered Ben's hands on me, his warm breath on my skin, his whispered words in my ear.

The damn text alert beeped again, startling me out of my increasingly erotic thoughts. I grabbed for the phone, locating it under the other pillow on the bed. Seeing that both messages were from Ben I smiled and clicked on the messaging app.

Morning! Hope you managed to get some sleep. I didn't... Couldn't stop thinking about you.

I wish you'd stayed last night.

My body wished I'd stayed, too, craving Ben's touch the moment it'd left my skin. He'd nearly made me come in my pants when he'd kissed me goodbye, rubbing his own erection over mine through our jeans, and sucking on a spot on my neck that drove me wild.

Somehow, miraculously, I'd had enough common sense left to decline his offer to spend the night in his flat. He'd been reluctant to let me get a cab back all the way to Ten Mile Bottom, offering me to sleep on his sofa, or even drive me back himself, but I'd declined both offers. I knew if I set foot in his flat we'd be all over each other and there was no force in the world that could stop me. And I couldn't let him drive me home, and then all the way back to his place when he was the one who'd get up early for work.

But most of all, I didn't want to sleep with him before we'd talked. I needed to tell him what I'd done and why I'd hidden away in Ten Mile Bottom. He needed to have all the facts before he'd decided if he wanted to be with me. Back in rehab, as I lay awake night after night, my thoughts swirling in so many different directions, I'd decided I'd never build any relationship based on a lie again. And I intended to stick to it.

Come over tonight after work. We need to talk.

Closing my eyes, I clicked send. That was it. My happy bubble was about to burst and I wasn't ready for it.

Alright... Shall I be worried?

Ben's reply was instant. My heart warmed at the thought. I didn't want to lie and say everything was fine and he had nothing to worry about, but I didn't want him to be anxious all day, wondering what I was going to say.

I just need to say some things before we take this any further.

Did you kill someone? Is that why you're hiding in Bumfuck, Cambridgeshire?

I chuckled, tossing the duvet off and sitting up.

No, nothing like that.

Phew, alright then.

Later that day, I was sitting in the reading nook, my laptop opened beside me, desperately needing the distraction of writing to stop ansgting over the impending conversation with Ben, and most of all, his reaction. But I couldn't focus at all, my mind busy creating all sort of scenarios, all of them ending with him looking at me with disappointment and disgust, slamming the door on his way out. My chest got tight at every door slam, my breaths coming out as shaky as my hands when I tried to type a single word. In the end I gave up, pushing the laptop aside and staring unseeingly out the window. My anxiety seemed to calm once I stopped pressuring myself *not* to think about Ben. I let a few thoughts swirl around in my mind, but if I ignored them, they simply evaporated.

In rehab, I'd taken on meditation as part of my recovery process. At first, it'd sucked, mainly because I was too stubborn to actually try and do it properly, but when I actually gave it a go and listened to what the instructor was saying, I started enjoying it. I wished I'd continued practising once I'd left. It was the only thing that managed to fully calm and relax me.

Sitting up straighter, I folded my legs and wiggled a bit until I was comfortable. Right now it seemed like the perfect time to take up meditation again, even if for a few minutes every day. I closed my eyes and tried to empty my mind of all conscious thought. I focused on my body, examining it for any aches and pains and discomfort, listening to my own heartbeat for a few moments, then focused my attention on the outside world. It was warm in the room, I could feel the breeze from the cracked window over my head and an even warmer spot on my hand where the sun was touching my skin. I could hear the sounds of birds chirping nearby, a car passing every now and again, a dog barking, Rose's voice chatting happily about something I couldn't quite catch...

With a start I opened my eyes to see Rose and another kid crossing the road from her house to mine, Eren walking happily with them. As if sensing my displeasure at seeing them, Rose's eyes found me sitting by the bay window and she waved enthusiastically at me, then pointed to my door.

It was safe to say my meditation for the day was fucked.

With a heavy sigh, I stood and went to open the door. I was aware I was still wearing the clothes I slept in – an old, grey tracksuit bottom and a Green Day t-shirt – but I didn't really care. I had zero energy, or desire, to be hospitable.

The knock on the door came as I reached to open it.

"Hey!" Rose greeted me with a huge smile. I grunted a reply. Her smile didn't waver. "Finn, this is my friend Andrè I was telling you about," she said, introducing the boy standing next to her.

He was a little taller than her, but just as skinny, his brown skin in stark contrast with his blue eyes. His hair was cut short and dyed a weird shade of blue-green, and he was staring at me with wide, unblinking eyes. Rose looked between me and him a few times, but when neither of us made a move to greet each other, she elbowed the boy in the ribs.

"Be cool," she said to him under her breath, then aimed a glare at me. I decided this whole thing would end faster if I played along so I extended my hand to the kid.

"Hey, I'm Finn, nice to meet you, Andrè," I said, even managing a smile. Rose still glared at me, probably seeing through my plan. Andrè shook my hand, but didn't say anything, a slight blush creeping up his cheekbones.

"Can we come in?" She asked pointedly.

I stepped back, waving them in. Eren barked at me as she trotted by my feet, her own glare matching her owner's.

I left them in the living room and went to make tea like a good host. When I returned, they'd settled on the sofa, Eren lying between them, and chatted happily about something. Andrè stiffened the moment I walked in, and again Rose looked at me as if it was somehow my fault.

"So," I said, casually, distributing the teas and sitting in the armchair. "What are you up to today, guys?" I thought that was conversational enough and would probably break the ice, especially when I added a warm smile aimed directly at Andrè. Eren seemed to have forgiven me because she jumped off the sofa the moment I sat down and came to lie on the armrest next to me.

"Not much, we're going to the cinema later, but other than that, just hanging out," Rose said, slurping her tea. I shook my head at her, silently reprimanding her for having no manners, and she grinned at me.

Rose and I talked some more, and she gently encouraged Andrè to take part in the conversation. He started out shyly inserting a word or two, but soon seemed to relax and became more animated. He still had trouble meeting my eyes, though.

"So, Finn," Rose said in a break of the conversation, "Andrè's brought some books for you to sign." She nudged him with her elbow and he blushed furiously.

"I, um, you don't have to... Finn," he winced as he said my name, as if he found it difficult to address me in such casual fashion. I smiled at him and extended my hand for the books he was pulling out of his bag. "I mean, these are my own copies and I'm sorry they're a bit battered but I've read them so many times, and this one," he pointed at a paperback that looked even worse for wear than the others. "It fell into the stream once. I managed to get it but..."

Rose laughed, interrupting him. "It was hilarious! The current was really strong that day and he chased after the book screeching some nonsense, I nearly fell in myself I was laughing so hard."

Andrè ducked his head to hide his smile.

"It's alright," I said, reaching for the battered book. "I love seeing my books actually being read, not pristine in bookshelves, never to be opened."

Grabbing a pen from the shelf next to me, I started signing the books. I could feel Andrè's eyes on me the whole time, and sure enough, when I raised my head, he was staring at me in awe. It felt really weird. Not necessarily unpleasant, but I'd kinda left that life behind. I wasn't used to signing books and meeting readers anymore.

Most of all? The hero worship in Andrè's eyes made me feel like a fraud.

"There we go," I said, handing him his books back. "Anything else I can do for you guys?"

Andrè straightened in his seat, pulling his shoulders back and when he spoke, he was looking right at me.

"Was Leo inspired by your own experiences?"

I frowned a little, not because the question was inappropriate but because I wasn't fond of talking about Leo in general. Andrè was looking at me with such hope in his big eyes, such admiration that I couldn't deflect the question like I was used to doing in interviews.

"He was," I said, leaning back in my chair, my hand automatically coming to rest on Eren's head. "And because of that, he's the most difficult character I've ever written."

Andrè's eyes softened and for the first time since he'd walked into my house he seemed to relax and be himself a little more.

"I'll go make some more tea," Rose said, casting me a warm smile.

Neither of us paid her any attention as we talked about *Lost Silence* and what it meant to Andrè. Somewhere along the way, the conversation turned to writing, life experiences versus life expectations and how to be yourself in the world we lived in.

It was probably the most engaging conversation I'd had in a long time, and by the time they left, Andrè felt comfortable enough to hug me goodbye. My cold little heart might have melted, just a little.

By the time Ben showed up at my door, I was a buzzing ball of nerves all over again. The moment I saw him, though, standing on my doorstep, all handsome and smiling, pulling me in for an insistent kiss, whispering how much he'd missed me, all my jumbled pieces fell together. I melted in his arms, letting him kiss my neck and nuzzle my cheek, before I pulled him inside, kicking the door closed. He pressed me against it, caging me in, his thigh between mine, kissing me as if nothing else mattered.

Pushing him gently away, I licked my lips, chasing his taste, then met his eyes. The gorgeous green was nearly entirely engulfed in black as he watched me so intensely I shivered all over.

"We can't do this before we talk," I said, lacing my fingers with his.

He nodded and stepped away, our fingers still locked as we walked to the living room. On the sofa, he wrapped an arm around me and kissed my temple, his hand coming to rest on my thigh.

"So, um," I began, my hand shaking a little as I brushed invisible fluff from the armrest.

Ben didn't pressure me to continue, giving me the space I needed to collect my thoughts. I appreciated his thoughtfulness, but the more time passed, the more unsure I became of myself. The only indication he gave that he was waiting, patiently, was a little squeeze of his hand. The simple gesture grounded me, giving me hope that maybe it was going to be alright.

"I have substance abuse issues," I said, deciding to just get it over with. "I've overdosed three times, the last time resulting in a cardiac arrest, and surgery to stop internal bleeding and repair my liver."

I glanced at Ben, fully expecting to see a horrified, disgusted expression, but was entirely unprepared for the empathy in his eyes. It was as if he knew what it was like to be so unhappy, so lost, so fucking lonely that all you had left in the world were mind-numbing substances that slowly killed you.

Abruptly, he pulled me into a hug, squeezing me so fiercely I thought he'd crack my ribs. I didn't pull away, I hugged him back, clinging to him, to his sense of understanding, for dear life.

"Finn," he whispered in my ear. "My god, Finn." The anguish in his voice making my heart crack.

Ben didn't give me a chance to say anything else. He kissed me, the feel of his warm lips on mine, of his tongue insistently demanding access, of his hands on the bare skin under my t-shirt scattering my thoughts like a flock of scared birds.

I gave in.

I couldn't form a sentence even if I tried. I had more to say; I needed Ben to understand the full extent of my addiction, the consequences of my bad decisions. But right now, with Ben's lips all over my skin, his hands roaming over my body, pulling at my clothes, I couldn't think about anything else but how much I wanted him.

"Bed," I managed to say, swaying as I stood up, pulling him behind me.

He came willingly, wrapping his arms around me from behind and kissing my neck as we awkwardly made our way to the bedroom. Inside, I turned in his arms, claiming his mouth in a fierce kiss, pulling the t-shirt off his back, only separating for a second to pull it off completely. His skin was a velvety smooth golden brown, a light dusting of dark hair on his chest.

Pushing him down on the bed, I fell between his legs. Ben crossed his ankles on my back and pulled me closer, his mouth finding mine again. I could kiss him forever.

I bit his bare shoulder. The pale skin reddened in the shape of my bite. Ben made a noise, a soft growl, then scraped his teeth over the skin on my neck. It wasn't a bite exactly, more like a tease, but I felt it all the way to my balls. I bit him again, softer this time, licking his skin, trailing kisses and small bites on his neck, his jaw. He moaned, turning his head to give me better access.

My cock was pulsing, leaking, ready to explode from the slightest of touches. I had to calm down or I'd come before I even managed to get the condom on.

Shit.

I didn't have any condoms. I never thought I'd be having sex with anyone here. My libido had been pretty much dead for months.

Sensing the sudden stiffness of my shoulders, Ben slid his hands up my back and buried them in my hair, lifting my head to look into my eyes.

"What's wrong?" He murmured, kissing me softly before pulling back.

"I don't have a condom," I said with a soft exhale.

I fully expected him to push me away, but then a thought occurred to me.

"Do you?" I asked.

Ben bit his lower lip against a smile.

"I do," he said softly.

"Oh, thank fuck." I kissed him with resumed urgency, grinding my hard cock against his through our trousers. "Strip," I commanded between kisses, lifting my hips off his as he pulled my sweats off over my ass. "I meant you." Ben laughed and I bit his neck, making his laughter turn to a soft moan.

After some fumbling, we managed to get the condom from Ben's pocket, and strip all our clothes the rest of the way off. I reached for the lube I kept in the nightstand for the rare occasions I felt like relieving the pressure of morning wood, and placed it on the mattress next to us.

"What do you want?" I asked in his ear, nipping at the soft shell.

Ben arched underneath me, the feel of his naked cock rubbing against mine sending little shocks all over my body. I was already too close, and I wasn't sure I'd last much longer, no matter what Ben preferred to do.

"You..." He panted, his fingers digging in my skin. "Inside me."

I whimpered a little at his words. There was nothing else in the world I wanted more than to be buried deep inside him right now, but I was so turned on I was afraid I'd come on the spot.

"We don't have to if you don't want to..." Ben whispered, entirely misreading my hesitation.

"Oh, I want to," I said, resting my forehead on his shoulder and taking a few deep breaths. "It's just that you're so hot that I'll probably come the moment I'm inside you."

Ben's chest vibrated as he tried to suppress a laugh.

"I'm nearly there, too," he said, lifting my head off his shoulder and looking into my eyes. "But I want to come with your cock inside me, Finn."

Fuck, but the low timbre of his voice didn't help with my situation. I kissed him again because I needed him to stop talking. My body was about to explode with need and my brain was fogged with lust. I couldn't remember ever wanting anyone as much as I wanted Ben. My nerve endings were buzzing not from a chemically induced high or from a couple of shots of tequila. It was Ben, the way he caressed my bare skin, the way he kissed me, the way he whispered my name on a shuddering breath.

I wanted him, so much that I'd have done anything to have him right then.

With trembling fingers, I managed to put the condom on and lube up. I wanted to do so many things to him, explore his body with my mouth until he was a shivering mess; kiss and lick every inch of skin; have his cock in my mouth until he came down my throat. But I could do all those things later, if Ben would let me, because right now I couldn't think of anything else but being inside him right this second.

The tip of my cock pushed at his ass and Ben arched his back with a soft whimper. I eased inside him slowly, sweat gathering on my forehead from the intense concentration. God, he felt so fucking good! Tight and hot and so damn sexy.

"You alright?" I asked when I was fully inside him, my voice barely above a whisper.

"Fuck, Finn," Ben said with a groan. "You feel so good, baby. Please move... I need you to move..." He rolled his hips underneath me, his feet digging into my thighs.

I was happy to oblige. I started moving inside him, slowly at first, giving him time to adjust, but when his fingers dug into my ass and he pulled me in more insistently, I knew he needed more. Quickening my pace, I slammed into him harder, making him groan, and buck his hips, and chant my name like a prayer.

I wasn't prepared for the force of my orgasm. It blindsided me, not giving me a chance to stop it. It felt like my whole body was on fire while simultaneously shivering from the cold. The intensity of the feeling rendered me deaf and blind for a long moment, and I slumped on top of Ben, distantly aware of his arms going tight around me, and his voice whispering in my ear.

Once I could move again, I eased out of him, discarding the condom. Ben was still hard, his cock leaving a wet trail on his stomach. He wrapped his long fingers around it, giving it a few tugs before I gently removed his hand and replaced it with my mouth. I knew Ben was as desperate as I'd been to come, so I didn't tease him. I swallowed his cock as deep as I could, and lifted my eyes to look at him. He was watching me with hooded eyes, his hands burying in my hair as he urged me to suck him faster.

"Fuck, Finn," he said with a loud moan and a desperate buck of his hips. "Just like that."

His taste exploded in my mouth, and I swallowed as much as I could, letting some of his come drip down his shaft. His body trembled under my touch, his fingers fisting painfully in my hair as I kept sucking him, gently, lapping at his cock and his balls until every touch made him wince.

"Come here," he said, pulling me up his body.

He kissed me as intensely as if we were just getting started instead of coming down from the high.

"That was amazing," he whispered, sleep already sneaking into his words. "You're amazing." He kissed my lips, my cheeks, my nose, the corner of my mouth. I felt worshiped and cherished, safe and accepted as I dozed off in his arms.

In the gloom of the evening, Ben's green eyes shone like a cat's. After a quick nap to recuperate, we were lying on our sides, facing each other, our hands clasped between us on the bed. My throat closed off just thinking about what I had to say, and I swallowed a few times to get rid of the lump.

"There's more," I finally managed to say.

Seemingly understanding that I was referring back to the conversation about my issues, Ben squeezed my hand and said, "Okay. I'm listening."

I tried to speak, I really did, but I ended up opening and closing my mouth without any sound coming out.

"Hey," Ben said, his fingers coming to caress my cheek. I looked at him, his cat eyes staring at me as if I was the most precious thing in the world. If he only knew how wrong he was. "I won't leave, Finn. I promise."

He couldn't make that promise and we both knew it. I could be about to say I'd killed people as I was driving high out of my mind, or I'd stolen money from charity boxes, or that I voted for the BNP. Ben's finger gently moving on my cheekbone brought me back to the present, and helped me collect my thoughts.

"I hurt people with my behaviour, and I knew it, but I didn't care," I said, images of Aiden, Renee, Dad, and even my mother rolling in my mind like a film strip. "The night I last overdosed was the day of my dad's funeral." Ben's hand moved to my neck, squeezing gently for silent support. "I guess I should say I don't get along with my mother. I blamed her for his death, and said things at the funeral I'm not proud of, but to this day I don't entirely regret." I searched his eyes, looking for judgement but I saw none. "So that night my friend Aiden and I... We went a bit overboard. Aiden would follow me anywhere, and I always end up dragging him down." I exhaled slowly, feeling the air ripping out of my lungs. I missed Aiden like crazy, but it was better for him to stay away from me. "We both OD-ed, I ended up in a cardiac arrest, and he had a heart attack." Every word felt like a knife to my heart, but I had to get everything out, let Ben know what kind of person he was getting in bed with. "Later I found out my sister had a miscarriage during the whole ordeal."

Ben gasped and I chanced a look at him. He was watching me with wide eyes, full of heartache.

"She keeps saying it wasn't my fault and that it was meant to be, and would have happened even if I hadn't OD-ed, but I don't believe it. God knows I've put her through enough stress even without ending up in the hospital. That was just the icing on the cake."

"You and your sister are close?" Ben asked, his finger so gentle on my skin that I felt my eyes misting over.

"Yeah." The word came out shaky, and to my horror I felt a tear slide down my nose. "She's my best friend. She'll always stand by me, no matter what I do." Ben's lips quirked into a smile before he wiped under my eyes with a gentle thumb. "She wouldn't have told me about the miscarriage, but Aiden somehow found out and told me. I've never felt so utterly useless and worthless as in that moment. It was the wake up call I needed to pull myself together and try and sort out my life. So, Aiden and I decided the best way to do that was to get away from London and its toxic influence. He moved in with his mum in Ireland for a while, and I came here."

I lifted a shoulder in a small shrug, exhaling in relief when the whole story was finally out.

"Thank you for telling me," Ben said, cupping my chin and kissing me gently.

I kissed him back, but my body stiffened, still expecting him to get up and leave.

"You're not gonna leave?" I asked, needing to actually hear him say it.

"No." Wrapping an arm around my shoulders he pulled me closer, kissing me deeper, stealing both my breath and my heart. When he pulled away, he searched my eyes for a moment, and when he spoke his voice was much quieter. "I started volunteering at the youth centre when I was given a community service sentence."

I thought I misheard him, but he met my eyes head on and I knew he meant what he'd said. Confused, I tried to sort through all the questions running through my mind when I felt more than saw Ben taking a deep breath.

"I'm not trying to make this about me," he said, reaching for my hand. "My point is, we all fuck up, Finn. What matters is how we handle the consequences of our fuck-ups."

I nodded, leaning in for a kiss. It was slow and sensual, and didn't escalate to anything more, but it was exactly what I needed to anchor me to the moment.

"What did you do?" I asked when our lips parted.

Ben looked away, biting his lip.

"You don't have to tell me," I added quickly. "Not right now. Unless you want to."

"I want to, but I'm afraid you'll think less of me."

A surprised laugh tore out of me. "After what I told you about myself? I doubt it."

He smiled ruefully, and didn't meet my eyes as he spoke.

"DUI," he said, closing his eyes. "I was drunk, but my mates thought I was the least drunk of us all, and should drive everyone home since we were broke and didn't have the cash for taxies, and I drove on the way to the club anyway. I didn't need much convincing, to be honest. We all jumped in the car like the idiots we were, but I lost control on a roundabout and crashed into the island, hitting another car."

"Gosh, Ben," I said on an exhale, cupping his cheek, silently asking him to look at me. He did, and the agony in his eyes tugged painfully at something in my chest. "Was everyone okay?" I was scared to ask the question, but did anyway. We'd started all this, we'd be better off coming out with all of it.

"More or less. I broke my arm and had a concussion, one of my mates bruised his ribs, but everyone else was okay. The driver of the other car came out without a scratch, but I'll never forget the moment I saw him opening the door, staggering out on shaky legs as he hurried towards us to see if we were alright. There was a child seat in the back of his car, Finn." Ben closed his eyes, giving me a short reprieve from staring at the agony swimming inside them. "Ever since that day I can't stop thinking about the what ifs. What if someone had died because of me? What if there had been a kid in that car?" Ben took a shuddering breath and I pulled him closer. "When my parents came to the hospital, it was the first and only time I saw my dad cry."

We clung to each other, fused together by sharing our worst mistakes. I buried my fingers in Ben's hair, massaging his scalp, his soft, warm breath on my neck.

"How old were you?" I asked.

"Eighteen."

I hummed, trying to imagine an eighteen-year-old Ben, drinking and partying and out of control, and failing. He wasn't much older now – only three years had passed since – but his presence was calm and reassuring to me.

"I had a hard time coming to terms with being gay," Ben continued, kissing my neck softly. "I acted out a lot, putting my frustration into drinking and partying and generally just being an obnoxious, stupid asshole. Josh wouldn't even talk to me anymore, and I don't blame him. I alienated myself from my family, didn't trust them enough to tell them how I felt."

"You thought they wouldn't support you?" I asked, even though it was hard to imagine that was the case after seeing Ben with his dad and brother. They seemed to have a close bond, something I envied.

Ben shook his head, his hair tickling the skin on my shoulder. "I don't know what I was thinking. I was an idiot. I came out to them that same day in the hospital and the concussion was the only thing that stopped Dad smacking me upside the head." I felt Ben smile against my shoulder and I instinctively responded with a smile of my own. "He told me I was an idiot for acting out all this time because of that and that he didn't care if I was gay. All he wanted for me was to be happy. Then Josh didn't mince his words, telling me what a moronic dickhead I was." I chuckled, imagining Ben in the hospital bed, his family gathered all around him, fully supporting him even when he was making mistakes. "And then Mum launched into a loud tirade in Spanish that made the hospital staff come running to see if someone was about to be murdered. The gist of it was pretty much what Dad had said – she didn't care about my sexuality, she just wanted me to stop being so fucking miserable all the time."

"Your family sounds great," I said wistfully, kissing Ben's temple.

He turned to look at me, his eyes sparkling in the darkness. "That's what you got from the story?" A teasing smile played on his lips and I couldn't resist kissing it away.

Ben deepened the kiss instantly, silently letting me know he was done talking. Wrapping my arms tighter around him, I kissed him back, all done with talking, too.

CHAPTER FIFTEEN

In the morning, Ben found me in the kitchen with a dreamy expression on my face. I was nursing a cup of coffee, leaning against the frame of the open French doors, looking outside into the garden and the fields beyond without actually seeing anything. Naked, apart from a pair of shorts I'd hastily put on after my shower, I enjoyed the feel of the slight breeze on my skin.

I'd left Ben sleeping in my bed, but soon after I'd come downstairs I'd heard him moving around and starting the shower. Now, as he approached me and ran a finger down my spine, eliciting a full body shiver from me, I was reminded of the night before. In the light of the bright, July morning, what had happened in the confines of my bedroom felt surreal. We'd talked so much, about our families, our friends, and our childhoods; about TV shows we liked and concerts we'd been to and countries we wanted to visit. We'd napped for a bit, then woken up to kisses and touches and soft, whispered words.

"Morning," Ben said, wrapping his arms around me.

I turned in his embrace, careful not to spill my coffee, and kissed him instead of a reply.

"Mmm, coffee," he said dreamily when our lips parted, stealing the mug from my hand and taking a sip. "Bleh, what kind of poison is this?" The disgusted face he made only made me laugh and claim my mug back. "It tastes like lukewarm, sour mud water."

"If you don't like my coffee, make your own," I said, gesturing to the coffee maker.

Ben eyed the old filter coffee machine with contempt. "In this?" He asked, so comically outraged that I laughed again, and kissed the frown off his face.

After a bit of grumbling, Ben made coffee so thick it barely made it through the filter. He still didn't seem entirely satisfied with it, but after a few sips he stopped glaring at the cup.

My stomach's loud rumble snapped me out of my Ben-induced haze – in my defence, he looked adorably grumpy in the morning.

"What shall we do for breakfast?" Ben asked, looking pointedly at my bare stomach. "I don't think we had any food last night, did we?"

"Nope, no food, but a ton of protein." I wiggled my eyebrows and nudged him with my foot. Ben smirked, and leaned over the table to give me a lingering kiss. "Do you know how to make pancakes?" I said when he pulled away.

"Sure." He shrugged as if it wasn't a big deal.

Last night Ben'd shared that both his parents had busy jobs, his dad running the garage and his mum working long hours as a doctor, so he and Josh had to fend for themselves a lot when they were kids. Ben's mum had taught them how to cook at an early age, and often, during the weekends and holidays, the whole family cooked together. Ben'd painted such a vivid picture of parents and kids getting along and having fun in the kitchen that I'd been instantly jealous. The most my family had done in the kitchen was argue over whose turn it was to do the dishes or make dinner.

"Will you show me?" I asked, and for some reason I didn't quite understand, Ben's eyes softened and he pulled me into a tight hug.

"Yeah, I'll show you," he murmured into my neck.

After breakfast, I could barely move. I hadn't eaten that much in a long while, and my stomach felt like it'd explode at the slightest touch. Ben must have felt the same way because he was lying at the opposite end of the sofa, an arm thrown over his face.

"Clearly, we shouldn't have made a thousand pancakes *and* eaten them all," I said, turning a little to find a more comfortable spot, but careful not to jostle Ben too much.

"You're a slow learner," Ben replied with a smile. I did jostle him then, entirely on purpose, and was rewarded with an unhappy groan.

The doorbell chimed, the sound reverberating through me as if standing too close to a church bell.

"I'm not fucking answering that," I said with a growl. "It's probably Rose. Or Ruby bringing pie, which would be a shame to miss, but I'm not eating anything for the next week anyway."

Last night, I'd told Ben about my unlikely teenage friend, her fluffy dog who seemed to like sleeping in my lap, and my elderly neighbours who had a more exciting social life than me. Ben'd commented that for someone who claimed not to like people, I'd been busy making friends all over the place. That'd earned him a slap on the bare ass, and turned into an improvised wrestling session, which in turn had led to the hottest sex of my entire life.

The doorbell's insistent ringing, and Ben's foot nudging my thigh, brought me out of the pleasant memories.

"Fine," I said, louder than necessary, hoping whoever it was would hear, take the hint and leave. "It better be fucking worth it." Ben's laughter carried to the corridor as I stomped to the door and swung it open.

Aiden stood on my doorstep, looking healthy and happy and fucking gorgeous as he smiled widely at me and pulled me in for a hug.

"Hi," he said, face buried in my neck. "Fuck, I've missed you, Finney."

I was too shocked to do anything but stand there, letting him hug me, letting his familiar scent envelop me, waking up memories I wished I could keep buried.

"You look good," Aiden said when he pulled away, giving me a once over. His gaze shifted over my shoulder, his warm, happy expression shifting into a frown. "Oh," was all he said, before I turned around and saw Ben standing behind me, his arms folded over his naked chest, and a confused frown between his brows.

For a few endless moments, the silence was excruciating. Then, smiling widely again, Aiden stepped past me and offered Ben his hand.

"Hi, you must be Ben," he said, shaking Ben's hand. "Finney's told me so much about you."

My shock started wearing off and my eyes landed on a duffel bag Aiden'd dropped on my doorstep.

"Um, Aiden?" He turned to look at me, his smile and open expression in stark contrast with Ben's frown. "Are you staying?"

"Yeah, of course I am." Walking back over to me, he picked up the bag and said cheerfully, "Now, where shall I put this?"

When Aiden got that perky, it was a defence mechanism. I'd seen him do it enough times to recognise he wasn't comfortable about Ben being there. Well, tough. He should have fucking called before landing on my doorstep.

I showed him to the guest bedroom, avoiding his attempt to interrogate me, and hurried back downstairs to find Ben standing awkwardly in the kitchen.

"I think I should go," he said, running a hand through his messy hair.

He looked so vulnerable standing there only in his boxers, his hair in disarray and his whole body tense. I couldn't resist going to him and wrapping him in my arms, kissing the corner of his mouth.

"You don't have to. Aiden's pretty beat so he'll probably take a shower and sleep for the rest of the day. We can still hang out as we planned."

Ben's frown didn't ease, and he looked away. I let go of him to give him some space, even if it was the last thing I wanted to do.

"What is it?" I asked softly, hoping he could be honest with me.

Ben didn't disappoint me. "It's just..." He ran his hands through his hair again, making it even messier. "I really like you, Finn. And whatever this is between us... It feels special. I've never felt like this with anyone before. But..."

I knew there was a 'but'. I just knew it.

"But, I want it to be just the two of us. I don't do open relationships."

I gaped at him, not entirely sure what he was getting at. "It *is* just the two of us." I reached for his hand and he didn't pull it away. "What are you talking about?"

"From what you've told me about you and Aiden, you guys did stuff together, and I'm not sure how his sudden appearance here will affect you. Affect *us*."

I waved a hand dismissively. "That's in the past, Ben. It's not gonna happen again. If Aiden and I wanted to be together, we've had plenty of chances. We'd never work as a couple, and we're both aware of that." I pulled him by the hand until his chest bumped into mine, and draped my arms behind his neck. "Trust me, I'm not cool with sharing you with anyone either." Ben's smile was slow but when it bloomed it lit up his entire face. "This whole thing between us may be new, but it doesn't feel like it. It feels special to me, too, and I'd never let anyone fuck it up."

He kissed me, as if to seal my words into a contract. I responded eagerly, welcoming his tongue into my mouth, his teeth on my lips.

"Does that mean we're officially boyfriends?" Ben asked, waggling his eyebrows.

I laughed, burying my face in his neck and inhaling deeply.

"Yes," I said, kissing up his neck, his jawline, his ear. "And I'm not letting anyone else touch you," I whispered in his ear and felt him shiver in my arms.

"Same," he said, cupping my cheek as he kissed me again.

"So," I said, flopping down on the bed next to Aiden. Lazily, he opened an eye to look at me, but I knew he was already fully awake. "What are you doing here, Aiden?"

He grabbed my arm and pulled me all the way down until I was lying next to him. His hand sneaked under my t-shirt, but before he'd gotten any ideas I pushed it away.

"We're not doing this, Aiden," I said, softly, turning on my side to face him.

He puffed out a breath. "Is it serious then? With Ben?"

"It's new," I said, carefully, as if treading water and one wrong move would make me sink. "But I'm falling for him, Aiden." To my horror, my vision blurred and I was on the brink of tears.

I didn't know why saying the words out loud I'd privately realised some time ago made me feel so emotional. It was stupid, really. Aiden had always been the one I told everything to, the one who knew everything about me, the one who'd seen me at my best and at my worst. Saying this to him made it as real as it could possibly get, and that scared the fuck out of me.

"Why is that making you sad?" Aiden asked, cupping my cheek gently as he'd done hundreds of times.

"It's not. It's making me happy." I smiled as a tear rolled down my cheek, and I hastily swiped it away. "*He* makes me happy. I'm just scared I'll fuck it up, like I do everything else."

Aiden didn't tell me I wouldn't, didn't offer any other verbal reassurance. With my track record, he couldn't. I wouldn't have believed him even if he had, and lying to each other wasn't what we ever did.

"Tell me about him." Aiden's eyes had always looked a bit sad, mainly because of their shape and naturally hooded lids, but also because something poignant hid in the hazel depths. But in this moment, what I saw in his gaze was beyond sadness. It was his heart shattering in a million pieces.

He nodded at me, encouraging me to tell him about Ben, and letting me know he didn't want to talk about whatever was bothering him.

So, I did.

I told him about Ben, everything that I hadn't managed to say over the phone. Aiden listened, smiling in a way that I knew he was happy for me, even if the sadness in his eyes remained.

"Look at you, so smitten," Aiden said with a teasing smile once I'd finished talking. I didn't even bother denying it. I grinned like an idiot. "Is he still here?"

I shook my head. "He left."

"I hope it's not because of me."

"He said he'd promised his mum to have dinner at his parents' house." Aiden arched an eyebrow. "Anyway," I said, playfully pushing his shoulder. "What are you doing here?"

Aiden shrugged elegantly, and his light tone of voice didn't match the sadness behind his eyes.

"I got sick and tired of the Irish countryside, and my mother force feeding me, so I needed to get away for a while." He propped himself on an elbow and smirked playfully. "I missed you. Did I say that already?"

"You did."

What are you hiding, Aiden?

I bit my lip against the words. Ever since we were fourteen Aiden and I had been inseparable, and had shared everything, even when it'd been hard or uncomfortable or downright shameful. If he was hiding something, he probably had a good reason, and I wasn't going to push. Not yet.

"So, you've been writing again?" He said with a genuine smile. I'd texted him a few times saying I'd been dabbing into a new story, but hadn't actually told him how far along I'd gotten. "That boy of yours must be one hell of a muse."

Was it Ben's doing that I'd started writing again even though I hadn't written a word in nearly two years? I didn't know, and I wasn't too keen on analysing it. I was just happy I was able to write stories again.

"I'm nearly done with the first draft of this thing, actually," I said, Aiden's infectious grin rubbing off on me. "I can send it to you when I'm done?"

"Are you actually asking me – your editor – if you can send me your manuscript?"

"Well, I haven't written anything in an awfully long time, maybe you've moved on."

Aiden sneaked a hand behind my neck, pulling me down to lie on his chest. I didn't resist.

"Never," he said, the rumble of the single word loud in my ear.

We talked for hours after that, catching up on everything that had happened in the last few months. In ten years we hadn't been apart for longer than a day, so it felt surreal to actually have to tell him all this. But it also felt good.

It felt good to have my best friend back.

My phone rang just as Aiden and I were loading the dishwasher. Seeing Ben's name on the display I involuntarily grinned, making Aiden roll his eyes.

"Hey," I said, unlocking the phone. "Miss me already?"

Ben's soft chuckle did things to my heart. "Yeah," he drawled. "Are you busy tonight?" He asked, leaving the 'with Aiden' part unsaid. "Because I was supposed to be at this party I completely forgot about and it's my mate Trevor's thirtieth. As much as I'd rather have a quiet night in, I have to go." He continued, not giving me a chance to reply, barely taking a breath as he spoke. My smile widened – Ben flustered was an entirely new kink I was thoroughly enjoying. "So," he said in an exhale. "Would you come with me?"

It was quiet in the kitchen and Aiden was standing right next to me so he'd probably heard the whole thing. I met his eyes as he closed the dishwasher and started it. I really wanted to go with Ben, but leaving Aiden alone on his first night here felt rude. As if reading my mind, Aiden waved a hand in my direction, mouthing 'go' and heading out of the kitchen.

"I'd love to," I said softly into the phone.

We arranged for Ben to come pick me up in about twenty minutes and hung up. I headed upstairs to get ready, passing by Aiden's room on the way to mine. His door was open and he was lying on his bed, reading on his tablet.

"Hey." I propped a hip on the doorframe, folding my arms. "You sure you're okay alone for the night?"

"Of course. Go have fun, Finney, I'm fine. I could use some alone time after being cooped up with Mum for months, friends and relatives always visiting to gawk at the freak from London."

I shook my head a little, certain it hadn't been as bad as Aiden described it, but he'd always had a flare for exaggeration.

"Are you sure *you* are ready to go out partying?" Aiden asked, his tone growing serious. I met his eyes across the room, biting the inside of my cheek.

I'd been so sure I'd managed to hide my anxiety about going to a party where alcohol and who knows what else might be flowing freely, but at the same time I wanted to go out and have fun with my boyfriend. I was twenty four, for fuck's sake! I couldn't spend the rest of my life hiding in an old house, shielding myself from temptation.

"It'll be okay," I said, with a reassuring nod.

Aiden held my gaze, studying me, then hummed and went back to his tablet.

"Have fun," he called after me when I pushed away from the door and headed for the bathroom.

CHAPTER SIXTEEN

Trevor's birthday party was held at a club in the heart of Cambridge. When we arrived, a bit dishevelled, lips swollen from making out in the car and our clothes rumpled but hopefully tucked in the right way, everyone was already there. They greeted Ben warmly and introduced themselves to me before Ben'd even had the chance to do so. We were swept in a whirlwind of introductions, teasing jokes and laughter – so much laughter – without giving us a chance to protest.

The birthday boy, Trevor, took an instant liking to me and started introducing me to anyone who approached us as Ben's boyfriend, even if neither of us had actually confirmed we were together. When I didn't correct him, he gave me a dazzling smile and a one-armed hug that was a bit too friendly for someone I'd just met.

For a moment, I tuned out all the music and the chatter, and focused my attention inward. I looked for anxiety, for a sign that I was uncomfortable or annoyed, and didn't find any. It was really weird. I was used to being cooped up in places with lots of people I didn't know, and I knew how to handle myself even if I didn't much like it. But I'd always felt on edge, looking for an out as soon as the pressure got too much. Whether that out was the nearest exit, or copious amounts of alcohol, or something a little stronger.

Surprisingly, engulfed in the tight circle of Ben's friends, with Ben standing close to me, I felt content. I'd never seen these people before and yet they'd accepted me as one of their own the moment they'd seen me. I wasn't naive enough to think my natural charm and charisma were responsible for that. From the way everyone interacted with Ben, clapped him on the shoulder playfully and looked at him with affection even if they were teasing him, I knew Ben's friends were quick to accept me because of *Ben*.

Everyone but Ben and I got progressively drunker as the night went by. It didn't bother me when people were drinking – I'd never craved alcohol. And I definitely didn't need it to have fun. Ben seemed to be of the same mindset; he was having as much fun as his drunk friends.

We danced. A lot. Ben showed me a few easy moves, as much as he could in the dark crowded dance floor, and I followed his lead, amazed by how fluidly his body moved. And when he pulled me close to him, his hips moving in rhythm with the song, the bass thumping in sync with my heartbeat, all the air escaped my lungs. His eyes shone in the changing strobe lights, happy and excited, his lips warm and soft when he kissed my neck. I was sweaty but he didn't seem to mind, nuzzling my jawline and kissing me under the ear.

I was putty in his hands. He could have asked me to drop to my knees and suck him off in the middle of the club, all sorts of people around us, and I'd have gladly done it. Without a drop of alcohol, or any sort of drug to enhance – or dull, depending on how you looked at it – the experience, I still felt high on joy. Ben was doing this to me. With a kiss and a soft touch and a little jerk of his hips he was driving me wild, intoxicating me.

For a moment, it all became too much, too overwhelming. I needed a minute to collect my thoughts, and get some space, so I kissed Ben on the cheek and whispered to him that I needed to use the loo. He nodded and let me go, heading for the bar to find his friends.

When the heavy doors closed behind me, cutting off most of the sound from the club, my ears started ringing from the sudden silence. I swayed on my feet a little, feeling as if I was drunk, but knowing perfectly well I'd been drinking water all night.

Maybe coming here wasn't such a good idea, I thought. Maybe I wasn't ready. My hands shook when I ran them through my hair and over my face. A craving for something strong, really fucking strong, overwhelmed all my senses, like a red curtain of bloodlust. It was the environment. My messed up brain saw the club and the dancing, and the exhilaration, and wanted more. A chemically induced *more*. Because that was what it was used to. Pavlov's dog and all that.

I pressed my palms over my eyes, leaning back against the wall. I needed to get a fucking grip.

On shaky legs I made my way to the men's toilets and pushed the door open. The light was dimmed, but my eyes were used to the darkness of the club and the gloom of the corridor so I could see pretty well. There were a few half-open stalls opposite the door, and urinals lining the wall on my left. On my right, next to the sinks, two guys and a girl were snorting something from the shelf above the sinks. The girl giggled so loudly my ears started ringing again. Frozen on the spot, I watched as one of the guys picked her up and pushed her against the wall, kissing her messily, while the other fixed his nose and met my eyes.

"You want some?" He said, inclining his head towards the white powder still spread on the shelf. "It's good stuff." He looked me up and down with a leer. "Good price, too."

I couldn't move. I couldn't breathe. I couldn't utter a single word because all I wanted to say was 'yes'. A big fucking yes. My heartbeat quickened with a sudden jolt, pulling me out of my daze.

TEN MILE BOTTOM

Not giving my traitorous brain a chance to ruin me, I turned on my heel and ran. Still in a daze, I didn't realise I was running in the other direction until I reached a locked door with STAFF ONLY written in big, silver letters. My hands shook violently as I reached for the handle again and again, pressing it, not sure why I wanted to get in that room but determined to do it. My legs nearly gave out when I spun around and stumbled in the other direction, hand touching the wall for support.

The sound of a door opening and closing registered in my mind and I headed in that direction, only to nearly collide with a solid body. I mumbled an excuse then tried to walk past him, but he stopped me with a hand on my arm.

"Finn!" I heard Ben say, then lifted my eyes to look at his face. My vision was blurry and I rubbed at my eyes, trying to focus better, only to realise I was actually crying. "Oh my god, Finn, what happened?" Ben supported my body with an arm around the waist and helped me walk towards the door.

"I need some air," I managed to say, my voice hoarse.

Ben slipped his hand in mine and we walked out of the club. The fresh night air made me feel instantly better. We walked further down the street to get away from the entrance, relief washing over me the further away we got from the club.

"What happened?" Ben asked, quietly, but I could hear the concern in his voice.

I slumped against the wall, crouching down, hugging my legs. I took a moment to formulate my thoughts. It wasn't just about the drugs in the toilet. That had been the cherry on the cake. The rest of the cake was built on layers of insecurity, cravings, flashbacks to a time I had no desire to return to, and an all-consuming need to feel happy.

How was I supposed to explain all this?

"There were people doing drugs in the toilet," I finally said, deciding to cut straight to the grand finale. "And they offered me." I lifted a shoulder in a shrug as if it wasn't such a big deal, but Ben knew better than that. He cursed under his breath, then slumped down next to me. I winced, not wanting him to sit on the dirty pavement, but didn't have the energy to get up. "I didn't take it," I added hastily.

"I'm sorry," he said, touching my arm to get my attention. "I'm really fucking sorry, Finn."

I scoffed ungracefully. "It's not your fault. It's what happens in clubs. Even if you don't drink or do drugs, you can't help but see people around you getting their fix."

Ben didn't say anything for a long while, but his presence alone was enough to clear the fog in my head and calm me down. I knew he must be blaming himself because he was the one who invited me tonight, and it was ridiculous.

I sighed and put my head on his shoulder. "I can't hide in that house anymore," I said, more to myself than him. "I want to go out and have fun, and *do* something with my life. I'm so sick and tired of being stuck in the utter apathy in my head."

Ben put his head on top of mine, his hand coming to caress my cheek.

"Stay with me tonight?"

I nodded, turning to kiss his palm.

We kissed for what seemed like hours. Naked, spread out on Ben's bed, I felt like there wasn't a spot on my skin he hadn't kissed.

"Come here," I whispered, strangely emotional over the slow way he made love to me. I didn't think I'd had that with anyone before.

Ben kissed his way up my body, making me shiver under his touch. When he lay next to me, I wrapped myself around him, twining our legs, our arms, our fingers. I kissed him slowly, revelling in the feeling of his wet tongue playing with mine, his soft lips sucking on mine.

"I want you, Ben," I said, gasping as he sucked on the pulse point on my neck.

He seemed to know what I meant. Stretching over me to reach in the night stand, he pulled out condoms and a bottle of lube. I shook my head slightly.

"I don't want the lube tonight."

Ben paused mid-move, holding my steady gaze, studying me. It was dark in the room, the dim half moon the only source of light coming through the window, but I could see a shadow of concern passing through Ben's features.

"Are you sure?"

I nodded, taking the lube out of his hand and turning to place it back on the night stand. He didn't let me turn back towards him, but pushed me onto my belly instead, hovering above me on his hands and knees.

"Alright," he whispered in my ear, his voice low. "But I'll have to find other ways to loosen you up." He bit my neck, nowhere near enough to hurt, then kissed the spot. "I won't hurt you, Finn."

I buried my face in the pillow, too ashamed to look at him. He'd seen through my plan so easily. I didn't need him to hurt me, exactly, but I needed something to anchor me to the moment; something to free me from that surreal feeling still lingering after the encounter in the club's bathroom. Before, a hard fuck with a stranger was always on the agenda after I'd had my hit. Sometimes, the guy had been so rough I could barely walk the next day.

I should have known Ben would never act like any of those faceless guys I'd fucked, and even thinking he would made me feel more ashamed.

I didn't have much time to mull over any of this. When Ben's tongue touched my hole, all my thoughts burst into a million colourful pieces, like a huge, shiny kaleidoscope.

"Oh, god," I moaned, loud enough to wake the neighbours. "Fuck, Ben, fuuuck." Face buried in the pillow, I tried to stifle my moans but it was too good. It felt like nothing I'd ever experienced, Ben's tongue soft and wet, licking at me, his lips sucking and placing hot, wet kisses on my ass.

I was going to come just from this, without even touching my cock. I couldn't remember if this had ever felt that good. I'd been rimmed before, but more as a half-assed prelude to the main event. Ben was eating me out like he could do it all night, and didn't need anything else from me.

"Ben..." I panted, barely restraining myself from touching my cock or bucking my hips against the sheet. "Stop... God, so good..."

I felt a little puff of air on my ass as if Ben was laughing, and his tongue was replaced with a finger. I whimpered, rocking against his wet finger, wanting more. Always attuned to me, Ben added another finger, curving them just right, sending jolts of pleasure through my body. I couldn't stand it; it was too much.

"Ben..." My voice sounded like gravel, my throat too dry to speak. I swallowed thickly before trying again. "Ben... stop." He withdrew his fingers, giving me a moment's reprieve. I panted into the pillow, too turned on to do anything but tremble, needing to feel Ben's thick cock inside me before I lost my mind. "Fuck me." I managed, folding my knees under my body, and sticking my ass in the air.

Ben smacked it playfully. I turned to look at him over my shoulder and saw him putting on the condom, then kneeling behind me.

"You sure?" He asked again, cock in hand, ready to fuck the hell out of me but still needing my confirmation.

"Yes!" I said on a loud exhale. "I've never been looser in my entire life, Ben. I don't need anything else, just fuck me already."

TEN MILE BOTTOM

Ben smacked my ass again, then slowly eased inside me. I watched him over my shoulder, fascinated by the way his eyes rolled back when he was fully sheathed. Even after his best efforts, it still hurt a bit. But I loved it. I wanted it. I needed to feel him inside me, as intense as my desire to snort that coke had been.

I needed Ben to overwhelm me, own me, make me come so hard I'd get off on it for days.

"Harder," I breathed when he started moving.

Grabbing my hip to steady himself, Ben thrust harder, faster, the feeling of his cock moving inside me dulling all my other senses. My whole world shrank to this moment, this exquisite moment of blurring the lines of pain and pleasure. I felt Ben's other hand on my cock as he folded his body on top of mine, jerking me off, the rhythm of his thrusts faltering. It didn't matter. I was high on bliss, of the feeling of my orgasm building inside me; on Ben's scent, his grunts and soft moans and the bites he left on my shoulder.

I spilled over his hand and on top of his clean sheets just as I felt Ben stiffen, his thrusts becoming jerky as his cock pulsed inside me. He panted in my ear, his hand milking the last drops from my cock. My legs couldn't hold me anymore, so I sprawled on the bed, Ben's weight on top of me.

Everything after that was a bit hazy. I think Ben cleaned up the mess as well as he could, managing to manoeuvre me under the covers and gather me in his arms. All too soon, my mind started buzzing again, demanding I overanalyse everything that had happened tonight until I drove myself crazy.

Feeling me stiffen, Ben tightened his arms around me and kissed the top of my head, the sound of his heartbeat under the solid, warm chest lulling me to sleep.

Ben held me as if I'd break. For the moment, I didn't mind.

CHAPTER SEVENTEEN

I slept fretfully, tossing and turning, and had probably kept Ben awake all night, too. When I woke up, his side of the bed was rumpled, empty and cold. My neck hurt, sending jolts of pain up my head. I sat up and rubbed at it, hoping to ease the pressure. It didn't work.

Swinging my feet round, I stood up, my stomach growling fiercely. I hadn't had a proper meal since the pancakes yesterday, and was getting dizzy with hunger. My jeans lay discarded on the floor, so I put them on, and, unable to find my t-shirt, padded to the door. As I got closer I heard voices drifting through it from the living room. Curious as to who was here, I cracked the door open and strained my ears to listen.

"You could have at least texted me you'd be here," Ben said.

"Since when do I need to text you? You gave me a key, remember?" Another male voice said. "It's never been a problem before when I crashed on the sofa. Why are your knickers in a twist all of a sudden?"

Ben gave someone a key to his flat? What was going on?

I fully opened the door and strode to the living room, running my hands through my hair, hoping to smooth it down. I was sure after the night I'd had I looked like shit, but I didn't give a damn. I wanted to see who Ben was giving keys to, and why.

Everyone stopped talking when they heard footsteps. What I found in the living room was Ben standing up in the middle of the room, wearing only a pair of sweats, his arms folded over his bare chest. His back was to me but he turned his head over his shoulder to look at me. His green eyes shone with annoyance.

I was sure it wasn't directed at me because sitting on the sofa, as rumpled and dishevelled as me and wearing only a pair of boxer shorts, was Ben's brother, Josh.

He met my eyes over Ben's shoulder and they widened for a quick second, before he smirked.

"Excellent," he said with glee.

"No." Ben's voice was firm as he stomped to collect the blanket thrown over the back of the sofa and the lumpy pillow laying on the armrest.

"Hey, Josh, is it?" I said, breaking the uncomfortable silence.

"Yeah, good to meet you officially, mate," Josh said, standing up and out of Ben's way as he fluffed the sofa cushions. "You're coming to Mum's fiftieth, right?"

"Josh!" Ben said, exasperation dripping from his words.

"What? You've been mooning over the guy for absolute ages, don't tell me you'll keep him hidden from the family." Josh's delight at the unfolding situation was completely puzzling to me.

With a glare evil enough to summon a demon from the depths of hell, Ben stomped past his brother, barely managing to keep the armful of bedding from toppling over. Josh grinned at him which seemed to annoy Ben even more.

"What's going on?" I asked, my head starting to pound in earnest. I needed coffee and food before I fainted from low blood pressure.

Josh lowered his voice and came closer, whispering conspiratorially.

"You've got to come to Mum's birthday party, man. Ben's never brought a boyfriend before and all the attention will be on you two, and for once nobody will be up in my business." Josh joined his palms together as if praying, shaking them in front of his chest as he spoke. The dude seemed really desperate to get me to go.

"And by 'up in his business'," Ben said behind us, strolling by, making exaggerated quote marks with his fingers. "He means not being able to remember the name of his date because he keeps showing up with someone new every single time."

"Come on, bro, you know how they are!" He turned to me, wide-eyed as he emphasised his point. "They have no boundaries, man. None."

Ben rolled his eyes. "I've never had a problem." He raised an eyebrow in challenge.

"Because you're the precious gay kid! Mum will smack anyone who as much as breathes in your direction with the barbeque tongs! And they know it."

"Or," Ben emphasised the word as if speaking to a child. "Maybe they like me because I'm nice and polite..." Josh scoffed, but Ben continued, ignoring him. "And don't actually mind talking to everyone in a civil manner."

"In a civil manner," Josh mimicked, mockingly.

I felt like I was in the middle of a toddler tantrum and I really couldn't take this without any coffee.

"Um..." I began and the brothers stopped bickering for a second, turning to me. "Is there any coffee?"

Ben threw Josh one last glare, then stomped past me towards the kitchen. Thankfully, Josh didn't add anything more to the argument and headed for the bathroom. Shortly after, I heard the shower running.

In the kitchen, Ben had the coffee already brewing in a sophisticated espresso machine that was lightyears ahead of mine while he made sandwiches on the counter top. I eased next to him, revelling in the smell of coffee mixed with Ben's natural, sweet scent, and placed a kiss on his bare shoulder. He turned his head so that I could reach his lips and gave me a little peck, before turning around to stop the coffee.

"So, what was that all about?" I said, leaning against the counter next to him.

Ben sighed. "Josh being a selfish asshole, that's what." Ben sliced a tomato with more force than necessary, then started arranging slices of cheese and ham on the bread.

"Do you want me to come to your mum's party?" I asked, tentatively, not sure what his reaction would be. The last thing I wanted to deal with was another tantrum, this time aimed at me.

Ben put the knife back on the cutting board and came to stand in front of me, spreading my thighs with his knee. I hugged him around the waist and kissed him.

"I do want you to come," Ben said, gently tracing my jawline. "But my family is big. And loud. And as Josh said, they could be a bit overwhelming and lack any sort of boundaries. I don't want you to feel uncomfortable being thrown in the middle of it on such short notice."

I nodded, not sure what to think. I didn't want to think Ben didn't want me to meet his family, but maybe he thought it was too soon. I couldn't deny I was a little disappointed, though.

Ben suddenly perked up, a smile widening his lips. "I know! You can meet my parents first, casually over dinner or something, and then when you come to the party you'll at least have met them before."

"Are you okay with that?" I asked, carefully, not wanting Ben to feel any pressure about introducing me to his folks if he wasn't ready, but I felt a tingle of excitement nonetheless.

"Yes, of course I am." He looked away for a second, a slight blush colouring his cheekbones. "I kinda told them about you last night anyway."

"Or rather," Josh said, walking into the kitchen wearing a pair of shorts and a t-shirt, towelling his wet hair. "Mum forced it out of him." Ben grunted, dropping his forehead on my shoulder. "She asked why he'd been so happy lately."

I could see Josh standing behind Ben, grinning so widely a pair of charming dimples appeared on his cheeks.

"Why is he still here?" Ben ground out, and as I wrapped my arms around him tighter, I beamed at Josh. He winked at me and headed straight for the coffee Ben had just brewed for the two of us. "Touch my coffee and die, dickhead."

Surprisingly, Josh took a step back, and busied himself with making his own coffee.

When Ben offered to drive me back to Ten Mile Bottom, I wasn't too keen because I didn't want him to have to go back and forth on his day off. But he insisted, and I was glad. I felt safe with him, and his presence always gave me the feeling that everything would be alright. I needed that today. As if sensing my state of mind, Ben reached for my hand and didn't let go until we were off the motorway and he needed his hand to change gears again.

Walking inside, I saw Aiden coming down the hallway. The rigid set of his shoulders set alarm bells in my head. When he neared, he took one look at me, and pursed his lips disapprovingly, trying hard not to lose his shit in front of Ben.

"What happened?" He asked, carefully avoiding eye contact with Ben and staring pointedly at me.

"Nothing," I said, striding past him and into the living room. I heard two sets of footsteps following me and then Ben sat beside me on the sofa.

Aiden chose to stand, glowering at us both. "Nothing," he repeated blankly. "So what about that text I got last night? And what about your face, Finn? You look like someone chewed you and spit you out because you were too disgusting to swallow."

"Wow, thanks, man," I mumbled, my mind drifting to the ill-advised text I'd sent him last night on the way to Ben's flat. I winced.

Ben turned to me, pointedly ignoring Aiden just as Aiden had ignored him.

"Do you want to lie down? He's right, you really don't look good, babe."

From the corner of my eye I saw Aiden flinch at the endearment Ben'd used, and I was almost certain Ben'd done it with the exact purpose of annoying him, but my head was still pounding and I couldn't deal with this.

"Yeah, I think I'll go have a nap."

Ben leaned in and kissed me softly, and then I saw him to the door. Making me promise I'd call him if I needed anything, he climbed into his car and left. Before I closed the door I saw the curtain of Rose's bedroom window move, and I gave her a little wave, knowing she was spying on me even if I couldn't see her.

Aiden was leaning on the living room doorway when I turned around, but I walked past him, mumbling, "Not now." I really needed a nap, and nothing good would come from an argument when my head felt like someone was kicking me with a steel-toe boot.

I woke up to the delicious smell of food. Disoriented, I needed a moment to figure out where I was and where the smell was coming from. It'd be too cruel if it'd been a dream.

My stomach growled in agreement.

Realising I was in my own house, and Aiden was probably cooking downstairs – although, exactly what he was cooking when he was as clumsy in the kitchen as me, I couldn't even being to fathom. Sitting up gingerly, I was happy to discover my head wasn't pounding anymore, and I actually felt half human again. Sleep always did seem to cure all my ailments.

I got up, took a swift shower – the whole time my stomach insisting food was more important right now – dressed quickly in sweats and a t-shirt, and trotted downstairs. Aiden was happily whistling to a song playing on his phone while he deep fried something on the stove, the apron he'd sent me fitting him perfectly. He glanced at me with a smile, before taking something out of the sizzling pot and placing it on a paper-lined plate.

"I knew the smell of food was the most effective wake-up call for you," he said with a smirk.

I stepped closer, peering at the stove. It looked like he was making tempura chicken strips, and another, bigger pot was bubbling on the other hob with nearly translucent, but very nice smelling, liquid.

"What are you doing?"

"Cooking, obviously."

"But..." I stammered, remembering a time when neither of us knew how to boil an egg. "How do you know how to do all this?"

I tried to snatch a piece of chicken from the plate and he slapped my hand with the spatula.

"I took a cooking class."

I blinked a few times, understanding the words but unable to imagine Aiden in any sort of cooking class environment. I also felt a little hurt he'd never mentioned it to me even though we'd texted daily. The realisation that for the first time in ten years my and Aiden's lives were turning in the opposite direction at the junction hit me harder than I expected.

"Why?" I said, clearing my throat against the lump appearing there.

"So that I won't be a useless twat who can't even cook a simple meal for himself, or others, anymore." He waggled his eyebrows suggestively, but if there was a double meaning, it was entirely lost on me. I was already salivating over the delicious smelling food and my brain didn't have enough capacity left to focus on two things at once.

"Go set the table, pour some drinks, and sit down. Nearly done."

I did as he instructed and soon Aiden placed a bowl of ramen in front of me, so pretty it looked like something out of an anime.

"This looks brilliant," I said, grabbing my fork and digging in. It felt weird eating Japanese food with a fork, but I didn't have any chopsticks. I made a note to buy some disposable ones next time I was in the supermarket. "And tastes so good," I added, my mouth full. Aiden chuckled, then motioned for me to keep eating.

He made tea when we were done, mixing several different kinds of teas until I was sure it would taste like spoiled milk, but took the mug he handed me anyway.

"So, what happened last night?"

No beating around the bush, then.

I sat in the armchair I usually favoured, blew on the hot tea and took a careful sip. To my surprise, it didn't taste that bad at all. I wouldn't say ginger and blueberry necessarily went together, but it wasn't horrible.

"Quit stalling, Finney," Aiden said with an exasperated sigh, placing his mug on the coffee table. "I need to know why you sent me a text saying you nearly took a hit, and then came home looking like shit." He paused, watching me as I set my mug on the table, too, then leaned back and folded my arms. "Did you take anything?" His voice was soft but dripping with dread.

As much as I appreciated Ben's support, he didn't really know what I was going through, and I was glad. I wouldn't wish it on anyone. But Aiden knew. He knew perfectly well the marks addiction left on your body and soul, the agony of the cravings clawing at you until you lost your fucking mind.

"Finney?"

"I didn't take anything," I said, then told him the gist of what had happened.

He visibly relaxed, sitting back more comfortably as if realising he'd been hanging off the edge of the seat.

"I'm scared, Aiden. So scared that next time I won't be able to turn away." Saying the words out loud made my stomach clench. Aiden nodded, looking away. He felt the same, I knew, but he had a way of internalising things before talking about them, so I didn't push him. "But I can't hide forever. Cutting myself off from temptation also means cutting myself off from everything I care about. From my own damn life!" I exhaled loudly, getting annoyed with myself whining like a child. If anyone had the power to change the way I lived my life, the way I saw the world and the choices I made, it was me.

"Does he know?" Aiden asked.

"Yeah. I told him before anything happened between us. I felt it wasn't fair otherwise."

Aiden lowered his lashes but kept watching me, the gold of his eyes sparkling under his hooded lids. I knew that look. He was about to say something that would break my heart, but needed to be said anyway. I stiffened, readying myself for whatever would come out of his mouth next.

"I'm moving to Tokyo," he said, tilting my world on its axis.

CHAPTER EIGHTEEN

"You're what?" I asked, my ears ringing so badly I thought I must have misheard him.

Aiden sighed, scrubbing his face with his palms. "I got offered a job two weeks ago, and although I haven't signed the contract yet, I told them my answer was yes."

"A job?" I spat the word like it tasted foul in my mouth.

Aiden had been my editor-slash-writing partner ever since we were no more than teenagers, and even though he freelanced for a few other authors and publishing houses, I still felt main ownership of his job. Which I fully realised wasn't fair, especially when I hadn't written a word in two years, but it still made me feel irrationally hurt.

"Yes. 'Walter and Brown' is opening new headquarters in Tokyo, branching out into manga, but also genre fiction and taking on some indie authors as well. Angie forwarded them my CV without even asking me, but I'm glad she did." Aiden leaned forward, placing his elbows on his knees and clasping his hands between them. "I need a change, Finney. A massive fucking change before I lose my damn mind."

Intellectually, I knew he was right. But that didn't stop my heart from breaking.

I tried to get my bearings before I did something stupid, like cry. Swallowing thickly a few times, I willed my tears away.

"I needed to see you before I signed the contract," Aiden said, so quietly for a moment I didn't even register he was speaking.

And then it hit me. He'd come to check on me, and if I'd been a complete mess – as I'd been for the first few weeks after I moved here – he'd have stayed. For me.

I was done being the rock tied around Aiden's neck, pulling him down, not letting him even take a breath before he drowned.

"It's a good thing," I finally managed to say, losing the battle with my tears, but smiling through them. "A very good thing, Aiden. I'm happy for you." I wiped at my tears with the hem of my t-shirt.

Aiden moved to sit next to me, and I was half in his lap by the time he manoeuvred himself in the armchair. Hugging me close, he swiped a thumb under my eyes, and then cupped my cheek, staring into my eyes.

"You know I'd do anything for you, right?"

I nodded. If there was anything in this world I was certain about it was that Aiden would always sacrifice his own happiness for mine. I never understood why. My own mother couldn't love me so unconditionally, how could someone else? But I'd accepted it as a truth that was an integral part of our friendship, of *me*.

"I won't ask you to stay if that's what you're hoping for," I said, and we both laughed. Snuggling closer to him, I closed my eyes for a second, imprinting this moment on my memory. "Will you still be my editor?"

"Of course."

I knew he'd said he'd always be my editor just yesterday, but I hadn't known about his new job then. I needed him to say it again. I honestly didn't think I'd want to write anything if Aiden wasn't the one to guide me, help me polish it and inspire me to write the best way I could.

"When are you leaving?" I whispered into the fabric on his chest.

"The day after your birthday."

That was only two weeks away. My chest felt painfully tight as I said,

"Go sign the contract."

"You're in love with him, aren't you?" Aiden asked without any preamble.

I looked up the from the laptop screen, his question jarring me out of the scene I was writing. I shrugged, as if it wasn't a big deal, but we both knew how huge a deal it was. Not feeling up to talking about it yet, I focused on my manuscript again.

From the corner of my eye I saw Aiden putting his neat signature on the contract laying on the table.

I was so close to finishing the first draft of my book that I could taste it. Lift-off was always slow for me, mainly because I wasn't a huge outliner. I had a goal in mind for the characters, and scenes jumbled in my mind that I tried to jot down, but other than that I let the characters take the lead. Once I passed midpoint, however, words started flowing faster and more freely, and I usually wrote the last few chapters in a day or two. Seeing the light at the end of the tunnel, I was eager to get down to rewriting and editing the mess it usually ended up being.

Aiden knew all that and had left me alone to write for the past couple of days, feeding me delicious Japanese meals, and taking long walks in the forest on his own. He'd even made friends with Ruby when she'd showed up bringing the most amazing toffee caramel sponge cake I'd ever tasted. Unlike me, Aiden was happy to invite her in and chat over a cup of tea. I'd heard him make an excuse for me that I couldn't join them but I was, apparently, under a tight deadline.

Ben was busy at work and we mainly chatted on the phone in the evening, which was definitely the highlight of my days. Even if I had to stop in the middle of writing a sentence, I did so at precisely 9 PM so that I wouldn't miss our phone date.

"Ta-daaa," I said enthusiastically as I plonked the printed manuscript on the table in front of Aiden. "I did it! I wrote another book!"

Aiden grinned, standing up to give me a hug and a kiss on the cheek.

"Good! Now we can finally have a normal conversation again instead of your grunting and far away stares."

"Ha-ha, very funny." I slapped him lightly on the arm and moved to put the kettle on. We still had half of Ruby's cake left and it'd go down nicely with a cup of tea.

"I wasn't joking." He winked at me when I glared at him over my shoulder, and pushed him away when he came behind me to peer at the tea cabinet.

"Go away. I'm not drinking one of your slush mixtures again. I want normal tea!"

"But..." He protested, getting cut off by the doorbell. "I'll get it. It's probably lover boy. He missed you soooo muuuuch he couldn't stand another second without you in his arms."

"Fuck off," I said, but couldn't hide my grin at his antics. He blew a kiss at me, then headed for the door.

When Aiden opened the door, I heard Rose's familiar voice carrying back to me. Aiden hadn't met her yet, but he had no issue charming anyone, so I was sure he'd be fine. In a few moments, I heard Aiden call,

"Finney, we have guests!" As if I needed a special warning or something. They walked into the kitchen, catching me just as I was slicing a huge piece of cake for myself.

"Hey, Rose," I said with a grin, pulling the chair beside me and offering it to her. "Come, sit down, there's cake." Rose looked confused for a moment, then turned to Aiden and asked,

"What's wrong with him?"

"I wrote a book!" I replied instead, throwing my arms in the air, still clutching the fork.

"Oh," she said, still uncertain. "Well, congrats, *Finney*."

I nearly choked when she used Aiden's nickname for me, and the bastard himself started laughing.

"I like her," he said, pointing his fork at her, dripping crumbs on the table.

It'd taken Rose no time at all to figure out I wouldn't like it if anyone but Aiden called me Finney, and I only tolerated him doing it because he was annoying enough to come up with something worse if I objected too much.

You don't like Finney? Fine. You'll be Slut Waffle from now on.

I chuckled at my own thoughts, and when I raised my gaze to look around both Aiden and Rose were staring at me.

I rolled my eyes. "Just eat your damn cake."

Rose had no intention of leaving like a good guest after I'd fed her cake, so she followed us to the living room, clutching her second cup of tea. She'd fawned over Aiden's idea of mixing different teas without any particular knowledge or goal, and genuinely seemed to like what she'd ended up with.

"Are you publishing this new book of yours? Because if you are, I really think you should re-open your social media accounts." Rose said, sitting down in my armchair.

"Why is it always you or your damn dog who take over my favourite chair?" I grumbled, sitting on the sofa next to Aiden, ignoring her question and the pang of anxiety it brought me.

"Eren is a shorkie – hardly big enough to take over anything."

I scoffed as Aiden asked, "His name is Eren? That's so cool! I love Shingeki no kyojin."

"Show off," I mumbled but nobody paid me even a sliver of attention.

"She's a girl, actually," Rose said.

"That's even cooler!"

Rose beamed, considerably distracted from her initial question, and they launched into a discussion about the anime and badass female characters, and then it seamlessly flowed into women's rights, equality and 'Time's Up' movement. I was happy to sprawl on the sofa and half-heartedly listen to them, needing the rest after the gruelling writing schedule of the past few days, when the doorbell rang.

"I'll get it," I said, but they didn't even register it.

"Hi," Ben said when I swung the door open, gathering me in his arms and kissing me. "I've missed you."

"I missed you, too," I replied, grabbing his head and kissing him again, deeper this time. Ben groaned, fisting the back of my t-shirt, and it took visible effort for him to peel away from me. "Can I come in for a sec, or are you busy?"

"I finished my book so I'm free as a bird," I declared, the triumphant grin appearing on my face again. "At least for a couple of days, and then I have to rewrite and edit, but you know what I mean."

"Wow, that's amazing!" Running his fingers through my hair Ben pulled me back towards him, giving me a soft, congratulatory kiss, full of promises for more later.

Ben must have heard the voices coming from the living room because he grabbed my arm and pulled me into the kitchen instead.

"Sorry, I just need to talk to you alone before we go in there," he said. I waved him off and asked what was going on. "Do you want to come over to my parents' house for dinner tomorrow night?" He tried to keep his expression blank but I could see he'd be disappointed if I said no.

Not that I wanted to say no. "Sure." I beamed at him and wrapped my arms around his neck. "Now that we've settled that, do you want some cake?" Ben grinned and nodded enthusiastically.

We walked back to the living room carrying our plates and mugs, and found Aiden and Rose still deep in conversation. They stopped talking when they saw Ben, and both of them smirked nearly identically. I sent Aiden a warning glare. If he called Ben 'lover boy' I'd kick him in the shin. He seemed to have read my mind and offered a courteous 'hello' instead.

"Rose, is it?" He offered her his hand after putting everything on the table, and she took it, her face beaming with delight that he knew who she was. "I used to go to school with your sister Maya, right?"

Rose confirmed it, then aimed a glower at me and my piece of cake. "Why do you get to have seconds?"

"Because it's my house!" I said tartly, clutching my plate.

Offering Ben my spot on the sofa, I took the footstool, and started eating my cake, unconcerned about Rose's displeasure.

"There's another piece of cake left," Ben said casually, aiming a forkful into his mouth.

I'm not sure who got up faster, but both Aiden and Rose bolted to claim the remaining cake. I shook my head, but smiled fondly as I heard them bickering and giggling from the kitchen like old friends.

CHAPTER NINETEEN

Ben's mum – Maria – greeted me as if I was a long lost child. Being raised in a conservative, tepid British household, I was completely unprepared for the warmth and affection she showered me with from the moment I walked through her door.

"*Ai, papi*, why didn't you say he's so handsome?" Maria said to Ben, who blinked innocently as she swatted his arm. "Come in, *cariño*, come in." She pulled me by the hand, oblivious to the helpless look I cast in her son's direction.

Maria was a striking woman, tall and slender, but with curves that probably still turned heads, even if she was celebrating her fiftieth birthday this weekend. Her long, raven black hair, huge dark eyes and incredible olive complexion added to the charisma of this whirlwind of a woman.

Walking into the kitchen, she snapped at Josh in fast Spanish, and with a nod of acknowledgement to me and a timid, '*Si, mama*' he walked out of the kitchen.

"Brats, all of them," she mumbled as she opened the fridge. "What would you like to drink, *cariño*?"

I asked for water and she passed me a bottle without any objections. For a brief moment I wondered if Ben had shared about my issues, but dismissed the thought as quickly as it'd appeared.

He wouldn't do that, not even with his family. An incredible smell wafted from the running oven, making my mouth water.

"So, Ben tells me you're a writer," Maria said in her musical accent, cocking a hip and leaning against the counter next to me. I nodded, taking a sip of the water. I was aware Ben hadn't appeared in the kitchen with us, and she'd shooed Josh away so that was probably the 'hurt my son and I'll end you' talk. "That is very impressive."

"Not really," I said, looking down at my feet. Ben'd warned me his mum wouldn't tolerate walking inside her house with our shoes on, so I'd taken them off at the door and earned a pleased smile from Maria. "At least it doesn't feel like it to me. It's the only thing I know how to do."

"That doesn't make it any less impressive, *cariño*." She touched my arm and smiled at me. I'd never known how to take a genuine compliment about my work so I looked away. "Ben's never brought a boyfriend home before." I looked at her to find she was studying me carefully, and ready to see through any false pretence I might have. "He really cares for you."

I care for him too, I wanted to say, to reassure her that hurting her son wasn't my intention. But I couldn't. As kind and affectionate as she was, I still couldn't let go of my own hang-ups about parent figures, and instinctively clammed up. She seemed to sense that, and thankfully didn't press for more. With an arm around my shoulders and a gentle smile, she led me to the dining room across the hall where the Goodwin men were busy setting the table.

Ben formally introduced me to his father even though we'd met in his garage, and they quickly found a job for me, too. I was in charge of distributing the napkins and the cutlery, while Ben and his dad helped Maria with bringing the dishes from the kitchen. Josh sprawled on the sofa with a motoring magazine, earning another scolding from his mother.

The evening passed in a blur of amazing food – roast lamb, roast potatoes with garlic and rosemary, a huge bowl of fresh salad and the most incredible raspberry cheesecake for dessert – engaging conversation, and a lot of laughter. Ben and Josh bickered like a pair of six-year-olds, and pouted when their mother told them off. I had to bite the inside of my cheek against a smile on more than one occasion.

Ben pressed his foot against mine under the table, in a silent show of support. The small gesture meant more to me than he'd ever know. Looking at the way his dad stared lovingly at his wife, his green eyes, so much like Ben's, twinkling with affection as he touched her hand or gave her a quick hug, I knew where Ben'd gotten his kind heart from. Josh seemed to have inherited more their mum's fiery personality, while Ben was as gentle as his dad; a strong, solid wall of support I could always lean on.

The whole family saw me to the door when it was time for me to go, Maria hugging me tightly and making me promise I'd come to her birthday party, and Bob shaking my hand and clasping my shoulder with a warm smile. Ben was going to drop me off on his way home, and even though my Spanish was basic, I understood when his mum asked him to stay there instead of driving back to Cambridge that late. Kissing her cheek, Ben declined, his voice sounding lower and sexier when he spoke in Spanish.

In the car, a strange sense of melancholy blanketed my thoughts. Why couldn't I have a family like that? As a child I'd wished for playdates with my friends, big birthday parties, laughter instead of shouting, a dog to play with, parents who held hands when we went for a walk instead of barely tolerating each other's presence. I never got any of those things, for various reasons, but mostly because my mother thought it was stupid, messy, or too much hassle.

"Hey," Ben said, reaching for my hand and clasping our palms together. "You okay?"

"Yeah. I was just thinking how great your family is."

Ben snorted. "Right."

"You should really appreciate them more. You don't know what it's like to be caught in the middle of a fight between your parents every day, and forced to choose sides." I realised my tone was harsh and Ben didn't deserve it, but a wave of anger and resentment always rolled through me when I thought about my childhood.

"I'm sorry," Ben said, squeezing my hand.

I'd told Ben the gist of my family drama, how I didn't get along with Mum, how Dad had died and how Renee was the only person with the same last name I could talk to, but I'd been too embarrassed to share the full extent of the rift with my mother. Most people didn't get it. *She is your mother*, they'd say, *how could you treat her like that*? How could I, indeed? It wasn't like she'd emotionally abused me my entire life, right?

"Finn," Ben said, too loud for the quiet in the car, and when I looked at him I realised he'd parked in front of my house and must have called me a few times before I actually heard him.

"Sorry." I puffed out a breath and leaned back in the seat, trying to stop the direction my thoughts were spiralling in. "Do you want to stay here tonight?" I asked. Ben hesitated. "Aiden is all the way down the hall, plus I don't really care if he hears anything."

Ben smiled, and turned off the engine. "Alright. As long as you have a spare toothbrush, I'm all yours." He leaned over the middle console and kissed me. "It'll save me an hour commute in the morning so we can have a lie in."

I really liked that idea.

We stumbled into my room, shushing each other and stifling laughter. I felt like a teenager trying to sneak a guy in my room again. Ben barely gave me a chance to close the door behind us before he caged me against the wall, plunging his tongue into my mouth. The kiss was anything but gentle; it felt like Ben was staking a claim on me and I loved it. I moaned helplessly, letting him know how much I liked it when he became a bit aggressive. Getting the hint, Ben pushed my t-shirt up my chest, pinching my nipples hard as he continued to kiss me. With a loud whimper, I took the t-shirt all the way off, grabbing Ben's head between my hands and bringing his mouth back to mine.

"Off," I managed to say against his mouth, clawing at the fabric on his back.

Swiftly, Ben removed his t-shirt, turning me around with one fluid motion. I gasped as my chest hit the wall, supporting my weight on my hands. With jerky, impatient movements, Ben managed to pull my jeans down, enough to expose my ass but left them around my thighs. He bit my jaw, my neck, my shoulder, then I felt the wet heat of his tongue travel down my spine until it reached my ass. He bit my ass cheeks, spreading them open with rough hands, flattening his tongue between them.

I cried out, not caring if I was too loud. My mind was blank apart from the sensation of Ben's tongue. My cock was hard to a point where I was scared to touch it in case a single stroke made me come.

"Ben..." I moaned his name in a desperate, frustrated exhale. "Ben, I can't... I want..." I licked my lips, trying to find the right words to articulate what I wanted, but Ben's hands roaming my body, his talented tongue licking my hole and the sexy noises he made drove me wild. I needed him to fuck me before I combusted with frustration.

"I've got you, babe," Ben whispered in my ear, his voice trembling with arousal. "Get on the bed."

"No!" I wanted a hot, fast fuck against the wall more than I'd ever wanted anything. And the fact that I was with Ben, with my calm, gentle Ben who became a beast once we closed the bedroom door, made me feel safe and wanted. "Here. Please."

Turning my head to look at him, I saw him hesitate but then he claimed my mouth again in a searing kiss that made me buck my hips against the wall looking for any sort of friction to ease the tension in my balls. I heard his belt buckle snap open, and Ben pulled away for a few moments before he plastered himself against my back again.

"The condom is lubed," he said in my ear, sucking the lobe into his mouth.

"I don't care, just fuck me already."

Ben bit my neck as if saying *he* cared, but didn't waste too much time before he slid inside me. I bent my knees to compensate the small height difference and give Ben a better access. I was rewarded with a sharp thrust of his hips that made stars explode behind my eyes. It was perfect. This moment, Ben, the way he moved expertly inside me, his fingers clutching my hips leaving red imprints on my skin. Our laboured breathing, our moans and pleas for more, faster, harder, don't stop; his hands on my chest, pulling me impossibly closer as he kept thrusting inside me.

With an aching whimper, I curved my back just so and grabbed for my cock, moving my fist in time with Ben's thrusts. A shot of heat clenched at my gut and I was coming with Ben's name on my lips, reaching behind with my free hand to tangle my fingers in his hair. He rested his forehead on my shoulder and I felt his shudder behind me, his nails digging in my skin as he clutched at my hip.

I smiled, happy and content with Ben's hair between my fingers, his smell all around me, his hammering heartbeat against my back. He breathed heavily against my skin, his breath burning a pattern there I'd never be able to erase. That was it for me. I was completely and utterly in love with that man.

Ben was sleeping quietly next to me, but for some reason I couldn't. I was tired, maybe too tired to sleep calmly.

A noise coming from downstairs startled me. I glanced at Ben, but he didn't stir. Thinking about it, I very much doubted someone was trying to rob me, with two cars parked in the driveway, and the reputation of an old dump the house had. Then it occurred to me that it'd been very quiet in the house when we'd gotten back, and I hadn't heard a peep from Aiden's room. Which was odd; he usually got up several times during the night to use the toilet or get a drink, or to stretch his legs when he couldn't sleep.

Slowly, I sat up and slithered out of the covers, hoping the damn floorboards wouldn't creak as I made my way to the door. They didn't, and the door opened silently so hopefully I hadn't disturbed Ben's sleep. Stepping outside in the dark corridor, I walked straight into a very familiar body.

"What the fuck are you doing?" I hissed.

Aiden laughed quietly. "Walking to my room. You bumped into me!"

I grabbed his arm and moved him a few steps away from the door.

"Where have you been? I didn't even know you were gone."

"Out."

I rolled my eyes but the gesture was lost in the dark. "Out where?"

"In town."

"With who?"

"Friends." He shrugged as if he hadn't arrived a week ago and didn't know anyone here.

I sighed with exasperation, pinching the bridge of my nose. Before I could interrogate him further, he pulled me into a brief hug and kissed my cheek.

"Go to bed, Finney." Sauntering off to his room, Aiden walked inside, closing the door without a second glance at me.

TEN MILE BOTTOM

Ben's parents' house couldn't have been more different when we arrived for the party. I could hear the music before we'd even parked in the driveway. Which, we discovered, was impossible. The whole street was lined with parked cars. Ben had to park two streets away. As we walked back towards the house I clutched at my gift, already nervous if she'd like it. Ben assured me she would – after all, he was the one who'd advised me on her favourite luxury candle brand – but until I saw her face when she opened it I couldn't be sure.

When we reached the house, I hesitated at the door.

"It'll be alright, Finn."

I hadn't slept well, weird, vivid dreams plaguing me all night, and I'd called Ben in the early hours of the morning, remembering he had to go in on a Saturday for an emergency repair. I'd caught him driving to work, and he'd put me through the Bluetooth speaker system in the car. We'd talked for a long time, until his voice soothed me enough to catch a couple more hours of sleep.

I still felt like shit, though. The stress of edits and revisions, meeting Ben's entire family, and the inevitable doom of my own impending birthday party was catching up to me.

As if sensing us outside, Maria opened the door, hugging both of us in turn. She was wearing a gorgeous red dress, fitted perfectly to her body, styled with high heels, minimalist accessories and her hair in an elegant braid.

"You look absolutely stunning, Maria! If I saw you on the street with Ben I'd think you're his sister," I said. She beamed at me, giving me an extra long hug, but only half-heartedly denying what I'd said. The woman was gorgeous and she knew it. Ben rolled his eyes at the exchange but I could see he was trying to suppress a smile. I fought the urge to stick my tongue out at him over Maria's shoulder, and I lost.

I gave her the gift and her face lit up as she peered into the bag. Ben smirked at me and raised an eyebrow in an 'I told you' gesture.

"Are you alright, *cariño*? You look a little pale."

"He had a dream last night he was being chased by a giant fish that was trying to eat him," Ben announced in retaliation.

Maria looked me over, genuinely concerned. "*Ai*, that's not good. Usually, dreaming of a fish chasing you means you're concealing some sort of emotional issues."

Ben snorted. "That doesn't sound like Finn *at all*." He added an expansive gesture with his hand and in that moment mother and son looked so much alike. When Maria turned to lead the way towards the party inside, I flipped him off. He laughed and brought me closer in a one-armed hug.

The party was complete madness. Loud music came from the stereo system someone had set up in the back garden, yet people still managed to yell over it and talk to each other. I could hear at least four different languages being spoken. Even in London, I'd never been to a party with such a diverse guest list. Maria's whole family seemed to be present, judging by the lot of gorgeous men and women and running kids, all sharing the same beautiful gene pool.

Instinctively, I squeezed Ben's hand in a silent plea not to leave my side, and he squeezed back. I shouldn't have been worried, though. Everyone I talked to seemed really nice, and everyone at the party was having the best time. People were dancing, or chatting in a less crowded corner, or eating and drinking. The kids were playing games, the adults letting them roam free, yet nobody complained.

My foot bouncing in time with the energetic song, I munched happily on a quesadilla, and watched as people danced. Ben leaned in, touching his shoulder to mine.

"You having fun?"

"Yeah," I replied instantly, my mouth still half full. "I really am." His green eyes shone even brighter in the sunlight, and when he smiled it was the most beautiful thing I'd ever seen.

"Hey," a familiar voice said, standing in front of us, blocking out the sun. I looked up to see Aiden, grinning down at me, and nearly choked on the quesadilla I was still chewing.

"What are you doing here?"

"Josh invited me," Aiden said, jerking a thumb in Josh's direction as if I didn't know who he was. At my puzzled expression, he added. "He was one of the guys I played pool with the other night."

Ah, of course. Aiden had befriended half the town, declaring he was bored shitless cooped up inside the house and going out – without me – nearly every night.

"Why didn't you say anything?" I left the plate on the table behind me, wiping my mouth with a napkin. Ben handed me a cold bottle of water and I drank eagerly.

"He only invited me last night, didn't see you today at all."

I'd slept in, or tried to, and when I'd finally gotten up, head pounding and in a mood to kill people – real or fictional – Aiden had already been gone.

"The party looks amazing, mate," Aiden said to Ben in an unusual show of friendliness. "And your family is nuts!"

They both laughed when Ben nodded in agreement.

CHAPTER TWENTY

We'd ended up driving to Ben's flat where he'd made love to me all night, taking his time, not letting me rush things. There was only one word that came to mind when I tried to figure out how I'd felt afterwards: worshiped.

We'd slept in, enjoying the fact we had nowhere to be on a Sunday morning. While Ben was in the shower, I decided to make breakfast. I wasn't confident enough in my cooking abilities yet, so I settled on toast and fried eggs rather than something more complicated. As I was cleaning the table to put the plates and cutlery on, a few pieces of paper fell out of a folded newspaper. I bent to pick them up, not meaning to pry, but I couldn't help seeing it was student loan application. It'd been approved on principle, but Ben hadn't signed it yet. Surprised, I opened the folded newspaper and saw a letter of acceptance from Pembroke College.

Ben had never mentioned he was thinking of going to school. The letters were dated a few weeks back, though. Maybe it slipped his mind. Although, they were on the table as if he'd been reading them recently.

"What are you doing?" Ben asked, making me jump and nearly drop the letter again.

"Sorry, didn't mean to snoop, but it fell out when I was clearing the table for breakfast."

"It's alright," Ben said in an unusually moody voice. "I'll probably throw them away anyway."

"What? Why?" I carefully tucked the letters back inside the newspaper and placed it on the counter.

"It's a long story."

I set a cup of coffee in front of him, and the two plates piled with food.

"We don't have anywhere to be."

Ben dug into his breakfast and I gave him space. If he was anything like me he'd be way more talkative on a full stomach. When we were done, we took the plates to the sink, and, still clutching our coffee cups, moved to the cosy living room. I sat on the sofa, snuggling closer to him when he joined me.

"So, college?" I prompted. "You never mentioned anything before."

"What's the point? Like I said, I probably won't do it."

"Why not?"

"Because it's just a dream!" He snapped. His eyes softened when he looked at me and he offered me his hand, palm up. I put mine in it, accepting his apology. "How am I supposed to tell my parents the life they've built for me and Josh isn't good enough? And prance off to college, leaving my dad and my brother to pick up the slack in the garage?"

"Hang on, back up a little bit. You're not making any sense."

Ben exhaled loudly, puffing his cheeks. "The garage is our family business. Dad built it from nothing, and you should have seen his face when both Josh and I joined him when we were old enough. I can't just quit."

"Have you talked to him about it?"

Ben shook his head. "But it's not just that. I don't like living here, in this small town, where nothing ever happens and everyone's always up in your business. I feel like there's so much more to the world, so much to explore and learn. The thought of growing old here without having been anywhere or done anything valuable terrifies me."

"I get it, trust me." I snuggled even closer, kissing his neck. I felt his pulse point beating faster than usual under my lips. "Aiden once told me that I only aimed for the highest point and anything underneath didn't matter." I smiled, remembering that conversation. "But the thing is, you have to go for what you really want, Ben. You have to at least try. You'll never be able to forgive yourself if you don't."

"It's not that simple," he mumbled, his pout so adorable that I couldn't resist kissing him.

"It really is," I whispered against his lips. Pulling back, I added, "As the king of overcomplicating the smallest things, I can tell you that it's very easy to internalise everything and convince yourself you can't do something. When in fact – in your case specifically – you can talk to your parents and figure this out together."

"I can't!" He said, throwing his head back on the sofa in exasperation.

"Of course you can! Have you met your parents? They'll do anything to make you happy, Ben! Remember what happened when you didn't trust them with the truth about your sexuality?" Ben winced. I hated throwing this back at him but I had to get my point across. "And remember what happened when you finally decided to talk to them? They stood by you, still do, every single day, and they love you. I can't imagine they'll ever stop you from chasing your dreams."

"I don't think they'll stop me," Ben said, but the conviction he'd spoken with before was gone. "I just don't want to hurt them, make them feel like what they've given me and Josh isn't good enough."

"That's not gonna happen." Ben looked at me with so much hope in his beautiful eyes that it made my insides melt. "You could walk in there right now and announce you want to be a pretty princess riding a unicorn and sprinkling glitter, and have your own show in Vegas, and your dad will be booking the plane ticket while your mum googles 'specialised unicorn stores near me'."

Ben snorted, then hiccupped, then out right laughed and pulled me close for a searing kiss.

"And I suppose Josh will the one providing the glitter in this scenario?"

We both laughed until our bellies hurt. When we calmed down, Ben pulled me over his lap and kissed me, fisting my hair, pulling it back to expose my neck. He latched onto the skin, sucking a what would become a purple hickey, then, satisfied, leaned back, looking at me with hooded eyes.

"What do you want to study?"

"Engineering," Ben said shyly. "I don't know if I'll actually be any good at it, but it's what I want to do. My dream is to work for one of the big companies that invest billions in new technologies and research. I want to help build something that'll change the world as we know it."

"Good to know I'm not the only one with grandiose plans," I said, arching an eyebrow. Ben pulled me down and blew a raspberry on my neck, making me giggle. I squirmed in his arms until he released me. "Seriously, though, I think you'll be great at it."

"Thanks."

We kissed for a bit, without any urgency or destination. We both seemed happy simply being together, touching, tasting. Ben's hands slid to my ass and squeezed gently, deepening the kiss, but it felt more like a promise for more, later, than any need to get off right now.

My phone chimed from somewhere, and reluctantly I climbed off Ben's lap and went to look for it. I found it in my jeans pocket, discarded on the bedroom floor last night. It was nearly out of battery, so I went back to the living room and plugged it in. I had a ton of notifications. Groaning, I started opening them one by one: a message from Renee, two from Aiden, a reminder to pay the electricity bill...

"I'm going to make some more," Ben said, shaking his empty coffee mug at me. "Do you want some?"

I nodded, still browsing through the notifications until a text from Mum caught my eye. She'd rarely texted me since I'd moved, stubbornly continuing to act offended in such a passive-aggressive way it drove me mad.

Finnegan, Renee tells me you'll be celebrating your birthday soon and supposedly want me to come, too, but I haven't heard anything from you, so I don't know if that's true. Call me if you're not too busy.

I sighed, my mood souring. With a frown, I pulled up my contact list and clicked on Mum's number. Might as well get it over with.

"Hello? Finnegan?" Her familiar voice sent a jolt of anxiety straight to my chest, but I pushed it aside.

"Hi, Mum."

"I texted you *yesterday*, why didn't you call?"

"I just saw it, was busy yesterday, didn't even look at my phone."

She huffed. "Just now? As far as I remember your phone is always in your hands."

"Not these days." A strange sort of calm always enveloped me when I talked to my mother. Or, rather, not calm exactly, but more like a protective layer that dulled the senses and helped reflect the blows.

"What are you doing these days, Finnegan? Wasting your time in that place, instead of getting the help you really need." She paused, I wasn't sure if it was to take a breath or reload. Probably both. "Please tell me you haven't started doing drugs again, now that you're without any sort of control."

"Because your control worked so well the first three times I ended up in hospital." Even though my heart was hammering and my palms were sweating, I managed to keep my voice cool and level.

"You know as well as I do, once you get something into your head there's no stopping you, or changing your mind."

"There are plenty of ways to influence me – *plenty* – Mum, you just never bothered to explore any of them. It was always your way or no way at all."

"That is really unfair, Finnegan." Her voice trembled, and even though what I'd said was true, I felt remorse bloom in my chest. I'd yet again made my mother cry. What kind of an asshole was I?

"Anyway," I sighed deeply, swallowing against the lump in my throat. "I didn't call to argue, even if that always ends up to be the case when we talk."

"And whose fault is that? I can't say anything without you twisting it and getting offended. When all I want to do is help you." She ranted some more about what an awful, thankless child I was, and what a supportive, wonderful mother she was, and I couldn't help but wonder if she was trying to convince me or herself. And, more importantly, did she really believe all that shit? It sounded like she did, which meant she had a serious case of tunnel vision.

I used a pause she made to take a breath to my advantage. "If you're quite done, I have somewhere to be, so let's get back to the point."

"Fine. What is the point of this conversation?"

"The text you sent me."

"Yes?"

I closed my eyes for a brief moment, then said through gritted teeth, "Why would you think Renee lied to you? If she said you're invited to the party then you obviously are."

"How should I know? My son hasn't called me himself to invite me, doesn't even want to tell me where he ran off to because I'm so unbearable that he can't even stomach seeing me anymore. What am I supposed to think, Finnegan?" Her voice quivered again and a sob escaped her. "But it doesn't matter, does it? Nobody cares what I think. My children can't even stand me, so I must be a horrible person."

I couldn't listen to it any longer. Not again. For my own sanity I needed to get off the phone.

"Look, I can't do this right now, Mum," my voice trembled and I hated myself for it. "If you want to come to the party, please do. I'll text you the address."

I disconnected without hearing her reply. Usually, she was the one who slammed the phone on me, having said her piece, but not letting me get a word in, and I hated that I'd done the same. My worst nightmare was turning into my mother, in any way.

My hands shook violently as I reached to put the phone back on the coffee table. I felt cold, and utterly numb. Every single thought in my head was screaming at me at once, like bloodthirsty animals, driven wild by the smell of a bleeding wound.

I felt Ben's arms around me and instinctively drew back. I couldn't bear to be touched right now.

"It's alright," Ben said, holding his hands up. "What happened? Who was that?"

I let out a sardonic laugh. "My mother."

For a moment Ben looked confused. I couldn't expect him to understand, given the way he'd been raised, and how close he still was to his folks. But I also couldn't have him blame me for the way I'd spoken to my mother. Not him.

"She was displeased I hadn't personally invited her to my birthday party, even though my sister had, so I called to invite her." My voice had grown cold and distant, venom dripping from every word.

Ben still had a confused frown on his face. "So... Why did that upset you so much?"

"Because every conversation with her upsets me!" I yelled, knowing I shouldn't be taking it out on him, but it was too late. The huge fucking mass of anger and helpless frustration inside me demanded to be let out, and there was no stopping it once it rolled down the hill. "She's manipulative and cruel, and refuses to even consider the possibility that her behaviour hurts people. Hurts her own children! And when we tell her that, she starts crying and acting like the victim because that's the easiest way out of any situation for her."

With effort, I cut myself off, panting. Frustration clawed at me, making me want to pull my hair, scratch at my face, bang my head against the wall until I bled.

Most of all? It made me want a hit so bad I could taste it. I could taste the sweet oblivion of not having to think about any of this anymore.

No!

The single syllable sounded so loud in my head it startled me out of my increasingly depressing thoughts. I became aware of Ben again, sitting next to me, watching me with so much compassion in his eyes it ruined me.

I started sobbing.

Big, loud sobs tore out of me and I was helpless to stop them.

"Jesus," Ben murmured, gathering me in his arms.

I didn't push him away this time. I was all out of will and energy to fight. He held me, drawing circles on my back with his warm palm, rocking me gently, kissing the top of my head until I was all cried out.

Once I calmed down a little, he pulled away, staring at me. I felt embarrassed, a grown man breaking down because of his mummy issues. Wiping hastily at my face with the hem of my t-shirt, I said,

"I'm sorry."

"Don't be." He pulled me closer again, his arms feeling so strong and secure around me I wanted to sob all over again. God, I was a mess. "Wanna talk about it?"

I really didn't. But I did anyway. "My relationship with my mother has always been strained, I mentioned that, didn't I?" I felt Ben nod. Understatement of the century, I thought. "I honestly can't remember a time when we got along, not even when I was a kid. I don't even remember a time when she'd sit down and play with me and Renee, or do something with us that was stupid and childish." I took a deep breath, feeling my chest loosen a little. "She claims I was uncontrollable and there was nothing she could do to get through to me, but that's not true. She'd try once, and when I – as the stubborn and obnoxious child that I'd been – didn't listen to her she'd just give up, or, even worse, she'd try the same fucking thing again and again. And of course, it always ended up being my fault, because she tried and tried and tried, and how could she make me listen when I didn't want to? I think I was thirteen when I started going out with friends, sometimes till the early hours of the morning, and she had no idea what I was up to, but she wouldn't do anything about it." I paused, collecting my thoughts. "I can't imagine ever giving up on my kid," I whispered, tears bubbling to the surface again.

"What about your dad?"

I scoffed. "That's a whole other mess. She'd moan about his lack of discipline, and then when he did discipline us, she'd yell at him for being too harsh and how we'd end up doing drugs because of him. Oh, the irony." Ben didn't say anything, so I thought he was too horrified to speak. "I never had any real relationship with my dad because of her. My earliest memories are of them screaming at each other, and every row ended with my mother in tears because Dad refused to apologise. Whether he had anything to apologise for, that didn't matter. She always saw just one side of the story – hers." I wiped at my eyes, the memories of my parents constantly fighting or arguing making my heart clench painfully. "Renee and I huddled in our room when the yelling started, trying to distract each other. But then when it stopped, my dad would storm out of the house and Mum would burst into our room – not to check on us, mind you – but crying, telling us everything that had happened in vivid detail, and then telling us in no uncertain terms we were supposed to be on her side because my dad was a monster who took advantage of her kindness." I felt Ben gasp but he didn't say anything. "The worst part? The next day she'd act as if nothing ever happened. She and Dad would get along for a few days, until he did something she didn't approve of and the yelling would start again. But it wasn't so easy for Renee and I to forget how much our mother had cried, and when we gave Dad the cold shoulder, she'd tell us off for it!" My voice rose higher, and even though I felt safe talking to Ben about this, my frustration started showing again. "It was what she always did, sending mixed signals, and then blaming everyone around her for not understanding. Wanting to control everyone to a point where we were supposed to consult her about every little thing and do exactly as she'd said, but not actually bothering to get involved in our lives. Not bothering to get to know her own children beyond the idea she had in her head of us." I pulled back, leaning against the sofa. Looking at Ben, I saw he was trying very hard to conceal the horror on his face and let me keep talking, to the point his expression looked like he was chewing a sour lemon and pretending to like it. "She didn't get along with her mother-in-law, at all, and of course, Renee and I weren't allowed any sort of relationship with our grandmother. Mum'd always been very vocal about her dislike, and when Renee and I messed up, she'd tell us we were exactly like our grandmother and despite her best efforts, she couldn't change our genes."

  I had many more stories to tell, like how she'd yelled at me when I'd given her a hand-drawn birthday card for her thirty sixth because the letters three and six were so huge everyone could see how old she was, but I decided I'd said enough. I could talk all day about my mother, as I'd done many *many* times in therapy, and still nothing would change. I wanted Ben to know the extent of how bad it was, because I trusted him, and he was my boyfriend, and it was a huge part of my life and who I was as a person. But even though I felt better and somewhat lighter for sharing it with him, I'd had enough talking about it.

"Why didn't they get a divorce if they didn't get along?" Ben asked, admittedly a question any sane person would end up with.

"Because, what would people say? She didn't want to be a divorcee. Plus, as I said, my mother has huge control freak issues. She still considers it a failure my dad died before she could change him." Ben scrubbed a palm over his face seemingly lost for words. I knew how he felt. "At the funeral..." I began, swallowing thickly. I didn't think there would ever come a day when I didn't get emotional thinking back to that moment. "I was so angry. She was crying and I didn't feel an ounce of pity for her. I blamed her for his death, I still do. I screamed at her in front of everyone, which is the worst thing anyone can do because random people's opinion is the most important thing in the world. I ran out of the service. I overdosed that night for what could have been the last time." A tear ran down my cheek and I didn't bother to wipe it. "The scary thing is, I wanted it to be. I felt cheated and resentful when I woke up in the hospital."

"Don't say that," Ben said, a sliver of panic crossing his face.

"I'm fine now, I appreciate the *fourth* chance I'd been given to sort myself out." I smiled through my tears, thinking how different my life could have been if I hadn't moved to Ten Mile Bottom. If I hadn't met Ben.

"Finn... I..." Ben came closer, so much emotion dancing in his eyes. He seemed lost for words, so he leaned in and kissed me softly, barely a touch of lips. We'd kissed until we'd nearly suffocated from lack of oxygen, and yet this tiny kiss felt the most special to me. He still wanted to kiss me after I'd hung all my dirty laundry out to dry. "Thank you for telling me," he said, not pulling too far away, studying my face as if wondering what he could say next to make me feel better. "And, just so you know, I'll always be on *your* side, even when you fuck up."

Seriously, how did this great guy end up with me?

I beamed at him. "How do you always know what to say?"

"Oh, I don't know..." He pretended to think about it. "I think I'm starting to unravel the contents of your messed up brain."

"Baby," I pulled him closer and placed a loud kiss on his cheek. "You have no idea how messed up it actually is."

Ben chuckled, his warm breath making me shiver.

"I think I can handle a kinky fantasy or two."

"Yeah? But how about a dozen?"

Ben laughed out loud, his eyes twinkling, and I was glad. I hated to be the one to dull the brilliant green as I told him about my fucked up family dynamics.

"Let's go get some lunch," he said, standing up and offering me a hand to pull me up.

My head was starting to pound from all the emotional crying I'd done; a walk outside in the nice weather and some alfresco lunch sounded heavenly to me.

After a long walk around town, we got some ice-cream from an Italian Gelateria, and sprawled on a sunny bench like lizards. Ben'd been quieter than usual on our walk, and I hadn't much left to say, but the silence was comforting rather than uncomfortable. I guess we were both lost in our own thoughts for a while.

"Have you considered that your mum may have depression? Or some other mental health issue?" Ben asked, the question ringing out like a gunshot in the warm, quiet day, and I knew why he'd been lost in thought. He'd been contemplating my family problems, trying to work them out in his head for my sake. Little did he know, the situation was beyond repair.

I licked my gelato, taking my time before replying. "Many times. Renee and I have talked to her about it, more than once, pleading with her to get help."

Ben turned to face me, his ice-cream nearly gone. "And?"

I hated the hopeful note in his voice. I'd been there, many times, getting an idea that could possibly help the situation, only to be crushed under my mother's stubbornness, and I knew how much it hurt to have your hope stomped on.

"She refuses to even consider she has a problem when it's clear as day she's at least severely depressed. I have a suspicion she also has some form of ADHD, and social anxiety."

Ben didn't say anything else, but I could see the questions still floating behind his eyes. With a heavy sigh, I said,

"In her head, she's not doing anything wrong. She loves us, tries to protect us, and everyone's being unfair to her. She refuses to even consider there may be another side to the story. And nobody can force anyone to get help when they don't think they have an issue to begin with."

I was really fucking tired of talking about my mother. I appreciated that Ben wanted to understand, wanted to be supportive and help, but I'd been in this situation since I was a kid. If there had been a solution I'd have probably found it by now.

Sensing my mood shifting back to the darkness he'd encountered this morning, Ben stuffed the remaining cone waffle in his mouth and stood.

"Come on," he said, extending a hand to me. "Let's go to the market and buy some food for a picnic, shall we?" I beamed at him, hurriedly finishing off my own ice-cream cone. When I stood he didn't let go of my hand, but drew me closer and kissed my nose. "And no more depressing family talk, I promise."

CHAPTER TWENTY ONE

I was thrown out of my own birthday party planning meeting. According to Rose, I was completely incompetent, and according to Aiden, I was in the way and should go make them some tea. Ben was the only one who stood up for me but the other two glared at him, so he shrugged and asked for Earl Grey.

Not like I minded. I hated organising parties, especially mine. Aiden had always done it for me anyway so why change the tradition?

I put the kettle on and took out four mugs, placing a random tea bag in each of them, only making sure Ben got Earl Grey in his. I was quite anxious about the party, already having second thoughts. Aiden'd sent the invitation by text the day before, so it was too late to back down, and I realised that even as I was considering a variety of obscure reasons to cancel.

Sensing my anxiety, Ben'd stayed over nearly all week, apart from the days he needed to be at the youth centre. Aiden had joked I should give Ben his own drawer, and I'd done exactly that, as well as bought him his own special toothbrush instead of the rubbish spare one he'd been using. I'd dated enough commitment-phobes to know one when I saw one, and Ben was definitely in the opposite part of the spectrum. He'd beamed like a child presented with a huge, pink candyfloss and hugged me tightly when I'd showed him his drawer.

Rose befriended Aiden even faster than she'd intruded on my own life. They hung out constantly, in my house. The damn dog barked delightedly as they played with her, and at one point I'd even heard some other voices floating around, when all I wanted was some peace and quiet to finish editing my book. How I rented a house literally in the middle of nowhere and ended up with a houseful of people every day was beyond me.

Surprisingly, I was allowed to go on the shopping trip for party supplies. It was the very last thing I wanted to do and I was happy to be excluded once again from the organisational duties, but Aiden was having none of it. He claimed I'd just moan about what they'd bought later – he was probably right, I was very particular about party decorations and hated the tacky stuff in most shops – so he'd rather I went with them and moaned during the trip. I made sure to show my displeasure at every opportunity.

The day of my birthday finally came, and I woke up to Ben staring at me with a smile.

"Happy birthday," he said cheerfully and leaned down to kiss me.

It was barely morning, the sun wasn't shinning through the windows yet, so it wasn't even 8 AM.

"Thanks," I mumbled, throwing an arm over my eyes.

"Quarter of a century, eh?"

"Shut up."

Ben shifted on the bed, then I felt a light weight land on my chest. Removing my arm and opening one eye I saw a black gift box wrapped with a gold ribbon sitting on my naked chest. Shifting my focus on Ben, I found him still grinning, watching me eagerly. He seemed way more excited about my birthday than I was.

"Thank you." I kissed his cheek, then reached for the box.

Inside, wrapped neatly in gold tissue, was an early edition of Lajos Egri's 'The Art of Creative Writing' which was the best book ever written on the craft, and which I'd lost somewhere during the move. I'd mentioned to Ben a few weeks ago how much I missed that book, and how much it'd helped me in my own writing, but I couldn't find a replacement copy anywhere, not even in the antique bookshops.

"How did you find this?" I whispered, unable to believe Ben had not only remembered what I'd said but went through all the trouble to find me a copy.

"I know a guy who knows a guy," he said with a cheeky smile. "There's more." He jerked his chin towards the box.

I peered deeper inside and found a gorgeous black pen with a Swarovski crystal on the clip, and two tickets for a show in Cambridge Arts Theatre. We'd walked past the building recently and the poster for the show had caught my eye, but it'd been too late and the ticket office had been closed.

"Thank you," I said again, pulling him down for a kiss. "You spoil me," I murmured against his lips and felt him smile.

I'd excused myself from helping with the preparations and locked myself in the bedroom. I had a few pages left to edit, and a scene to rewrite, and my manuscript would be ready for Aiden's expert editing skills. I really needed to finish it before tomorrow.

The first time the bell rang was the first time I actually considered who Aiden might have invited. Apart from my family, Rose, and a few other people he'd made friends with in town, I couldn't think of anyone else who might be coming. I shouldn't have worried, or doubted Aiden's ability to charm anyone into friendship. When I eventually went downstairs to join the party, the garden was full of people. The tasteful decorations I'd picked were all in place around the garden – banners hung off the fence, garlands and fairy lights weaved around the tables, chairs, and deck railing. People milled around wearing party hats, the only decoration I hadn't pre-approved, and seemed to enjoy the food tastefully arranged on the tables. In the far corner, the coal in the barbeque still smoked faintly, but all the meat seemed to be done and distributed around.

The music cut off when people noticed me and erupted into cheers and congratulations. I was oddly touched by the display of affection and happiness, considering I'd tried my best to alienate everyone in the past few months. Ben came over, grabbing my hand and we strolled together through the garden, chatting to people. His mother appeared out of nowhere with a brilliant smile so much like Ben's, and hugged me, not letting me go until I squirmed. His dad shook my hand while Josh clapped my shoulder, balancing a plate piled with meat in his other hand.

I saw Ruby and Steve, Rose and Andrè, and to my surprise a couple of other kids their age, playing with Eren and giggling. Aiden was hanging out with a group of people I didn't know, but seemed content enough as he waved at me with a wink. My eyes kept roaming around the garden looking for my mother and Renee. I saw them sitting a bit away from the others, Renee and Mum talking while Renee's partner, Luis, was chatting animatedly with a guy I haven't seen before.

"I'll be right back," I said to Ben, letting go of his hand. He followed my line of sight and nodded.

"Do you want me to come?"

"In a minute, okay? Let me test the waters first." I kissed him lightly on the lips. "I want to introduce you without any unnecessary drama."

Seeing me approach, Renee jumped out of her seat and tackle-hugged me. I stumbled back, laughing, hugging her tightly. Her wild hair tickled my face and I smoothed it before pulling away.

"I'm not done hugging," she protested.

"I'm not done living! You were squeezing the breath out of me!"

She slapped my arm. "And whose fault is that?"

"Yours?" That earned me another slap, but I couldn't hold my smile back.

Renee was five-foot-two at best, but so full of energy she seemed much bigger. Her long, blonde hair was always streaked with different colour highlights, and today they were purple, pink, and blue.

"Alright, let's go say hello because I can feel her staring a hole in my back, and then I want to talk to you in private."

"About what?"

"I'll tell you later." She grabbed my hand and pulled me towards Mum.

"Hi, Mum," I said when we approached her, sticking my hands in my pockets. I waved at Luis and he waved back, but he knew our family dynamic well by now, and he sensed it was safer to stay away.

"Finnegan, is everything okay?" She stood up, a head shorter than me but making me feel smaller than a snail. "I was worried you weren't feeling well. All your guests were here before you, and I thought, something surely must have happened to you."

I clenched my jaw and pushed my irritation aside.

"Nope, all is fine." I didn't offer any explanation, and she pursed her lips.

"Well," she said with an exaggerated sigh. "Happy birthday, Finnegan." She thrust a gift bag in my general direction, but didn't offer me a hug.

I was relieved. When we were younger, she'd pretended to be happy on our birthdays, overly excited and tactile. I'd never particularly liked when she'd hugged me, not even when we were kids, and she'd always taken it personally. But what annoyed me even more was that she'd refused to acknowledge the fact I didn't like to be touched, but kept doing it anyway.

The silence stretched as I spaced out, Renee's elbow in my ribs jarring me out of my thoughts.

"Thanks," I said, peering into the gift bag. It was the latest bestselling hardback thriller.

"So, um..." Mum began, uncharacteristically unsure. "Who's that young man I saw you holding hands with?"

A pang of protectiveness hit me in the chest, and for a brief moment I didn't want her to meet Ben.

"It's my boyfriend, Ben."

My mother arched an eyebrow. "Boyfriend? I don't think I've ever heard you say that word before."

"Well, I'm saying it now."

I could see her calculating her next words, knowing it'd be something that could make me lose my cool. She could aim her jabs at me all she wanted but I'd never stand her doing that to Ben.

"Why don't we go over there and Finn will introduce us, Mum?" Renee said, sensing she needed to interfere to deactivate the bomb before it exploded.

Turning on my heel, I led the way to where Ben was standing, talking to Josh and their dad. He was watching me when I met his eyes, as if he'd been willing me to turn and head their way.

"Mum, Renee, this is my boyfriend Ben, his brother Josh and his dad, Robert," I said, gesturing to each in turn. They took care of the rest of the introduction by themselves as I watched from the sidelines.

Ben's dad seemed genuinely pleased to meet Mum, especially when she conjured her public persona, smiling at all the right places, and saying the right things.

Maria materialized next to me, and didn't even wait for me to introduce her to my mother. She swept her in a big hug, talking a mile a minute, my wide-eyed mother rendered speechless for the first time.

I used the distraction to step away. Ben followed me, and we snuck out towards the kitchen.

"That went well," he said as I poured us a glass of water each, dropping a couple of ice cubes in it.

"I'm just glad it's over. Hopefully, there won't be any occasion for us to talk again, and we'll part ways peacefully."

I drank eagerly from the glass, my throat feeling parched and sore, absently wondering if I was coming down with something.

"Hey," Renee said as she joined us into the kitchen. "So this is where you ran off to." Ben smiled warmly at her, then kissed my cheek and excused himself. "I love him," Renee stage whispered.

Me too, I thought.

Putting that particular thought aside for now, I focused on Renee. "So what did you want to tell me?"

She beamed, unable to keep her excitement at bay. "I'm pregnant," she declared, clapping her hands together.

"Oh my gosh, Renee, really?" I felt my heart soar with so much happiness I wasn't sure I could handle it.

She nodded, still grinning.

"Really?" I asked again, needing to hear her confirm it.

"Yes, really, Finn! You're going to be an uncle in about seven months!"

I hugged my sister, suddenly all too aware she was carrying another life inside her, so I decided against squeezing her too tight or twirling her around as I usually did. My happiness didn't last too long, though, because over my sister's shoulder I saw Mum standing in the doorway, looking at us with a pinched expression, her eyes already misting over.

"You're pregnant?" She said, her voice barely above a whisper.

Renee stiffened in my arms.

"When were you planning to tell me?" Mum demanded when Renee turned to face her. I folded my arms over my chest, ready to jump to my sister's defence.

"When I was ready," Renee replied, her voice turning to steel.

"So, what, you were going to hide something so important from your own mother?" Mum's lip trembled, her eyes watering.

"It's not hiding, it's choosing not to share something *private* before you're ready. There's a difference," I said before Renee could reply.

"Stay out of this, Finnegan," my mother snapped at me, a tear rolling down her cheek. "Don't create arguments out of everything I say, like you always do, upsetting your sister. She already lost a baby because of you."

I took a step back, pain exploding in my chest as if she'd shot me. I barely registered Aiden's voice speaking nearby, taking my mother and Renee out of the room before it exploded in a fight this little town had never seen.

I slumped down the wall, burying my face in my hands. The impending headache pulsed slowly in my temples, gathering strength by the second.

"Finn!" I heard Ben call, unmistakable urgency in his voice. "What happened? Are you alright?" He kneeled in front of me, pushing my head up gently to look into my eyes.

"I don't feel like celebrating anymore," I said, letting the tears fall.

In the end, it was Renee who convinced me to stop sulking in my room and rejoin the party. Ben'd left me by myself after I'd asked him for some space, but he kept sending people to check up on me. I didn't ask what'd happened after they'd left me in the kitchen and Renee didn't volunteer the information. She only said Mum had left, and I felt relief so palpable it felt like someone lifted a boulder off my chest.

"Come on," she coaxed. "Everyone's having a great time, and it's nearly dark enough for the cake." She offered me her hand, and I took it, hugging her as I stood up.

"Thanks," I said, burying my face in her hair. "For this, and for choosing to tell me about the baby."

I'd never stop feeling guilty about Renee's miscarriage, but the happiness and contentment in her eyes gave me hope everything would be alright.

Ben and Aiden carried the cake stand together because it was too huge for one person. They'd ordered me a cake in the shape of a stack of four books – my three published ones and the new one on top. With a silly smile on my face I watched the two men I cared for most in the world carry my birthday cake, alight with candles, leading everyone into the 'Happy Birthday' song.

Placing the cake on the table before me, Ben came round to my side, kissed my cheek and whispered,

"Make a wish."

Closing my eyes, I held his hand in mine, reaching for Aiden's on my other side, and blew the candles, all in one go.

Later, Ben and I lay in my bed, the soft light of the bedside lamp making Ben's skin look an even deeper shade of olive. Propped on my elbow, I traced invisible lines on Ben's sweaty chest, still high from the way he'd made love to me tonight, as if sex was a religious experience and he had a lot of praying to make up for. Something had shifted between us as he'd stared into my eyes and moved slowly inside me, stalling my pleasure for as long as he could, so when I came I felt the world shatter around me, taking all my pain with it.

Even now, as we lay in each other's arms, I could feel something was different. Ben was more thoughtful than usual, his gaze turned inward as if he was contemplating something deep inside himself.

Gently, I placed my palm on his cheek and drew him in for a kiss. The moment my lips touched his, Ben snapped out of whatever was bothering him and he was with me again, body and soul.

"Everything okay?" I asked tentatively, not sure I'd like his answer. I had a suspicion he was freaked out by what had happened in the kitchen with my mother, as any normal person would be. Witnessing the extent of my mother's desire to hurt me first hand had to be upsetting for him, especially when he was the one left to pick me up off the floor afterwards.

"Yeah," he replied, kissing the corner of my mouth. Ever since that first time he'd done it, it'd become our signature gesture of comfort. "I was just thinking."

"About what?"

He didn't reply straight away, his gaze shifting to the ceiling again, but his warm fingers never stopped caressing my arm.

"You. Your family."

The drop of dread I could feel in my chest a few minutes ago expanded and burst at his words. Determined to hide my panic, I chuckled, the sound empty and devoid of any humour even to my own ears.

"You don't want to get tangled in that particular shit show?" I tried my best to make my voice sound light, and keep my body language as relaxed as I could, but Ben tightened his hold on me as if he thought I'd bolt out of the bed.

"Too late for that," he said, holding my gaze, his eyes shining more than usual.

"Never too late to run away from the crazy." I arched an eyebrow, my hand stilling on his chest. My heart pounded, loud and fast, as I waited for Ben to tell me he couldn't do this. It was too much, and it would probably never stop, and he couldn't handle picking up the pieces while my mother recharged her ammunition.

"It is for me," he said, bringing me out of my increasingly miserable thoughts. He held my eyes for a moment longer, then added, "I'm so in love with you, Finn." He inhaled sharply as if surprising himself with the admission.

I waited for him to take it back, to change his mind, to realise what he was getting into. To grin and tell me he was kidding. To get up and casually head for the bathroom as if he hadn't just turned my world upside down.

He didn't.

Instead, he drew me closer and kissed me, his lips parting mine, his tongue gently licking at my lower lip before he nipped at it and sucked it into his mouth. It was a teasing kiss, a kiss designed to break me out of my stupor.

"I..." I began, but my voice was so rough I had to clear my throat. "I feel the same way." I winced at the lame reply and felt my cheeks flame.

Ben laughed softly, tracing my cheekbone with his finger.

"Say it," he coaxed, gently, looking at me in a way I had no doubt what he'd said was true.

It took me a moment to gather the courage to say the words, but when I did I felt something inside me shatter, making my chest lighter and my breathing easier.

"I love you, Ben."

So that was what it felt like to say those words. I never knew.

I liked it.

CHAPTER TWENTY TWO

The airport was busy and crowded, people pulling their suitcases as they hurried through the throng of people. The lights and sounds of the place would be too much on a good day, but today I was hyperaware of everyone around me, of every touch and sound. Adrenalin flooded my body as we approached the security gates, making me shiver.

A comforting hand on my arm steadied me, the point of contact the only warmth I could feel. Turning my head to look at Ben, I saw him gazing back at me with concern, but the moment our eyes met he gave me an encouraging smile. He leaned in to kiss my cheek and say close to my ear,

"I'll say goodbye and then give you a minute, okay? I'll wait for you right outside the doors."

I nodded, too numb to do anything more.

In a daze, I saw him hug Aiden goodbye, clapping him on the back. Aiden whispered something in his ear, keeping him close longer than usual, and I saw Ben say something back. I was too upset to even try and take a guess about the exchange, but even in that state I realised it was a bit unusual for them. So far, they'd tolerated each other, but been apprehensive of one another, barely conversing unless they had to. Why they were so friendly all of a sudden was anyone's guess.

Ben walked past me, giving me a light squeeze of support on the upper arm, and then he was gone. Aiden stood before me, tall and handsome and smiling, and I barely resisted the urge to grab him, drag him back home, and lock him in my attic.

"You suck for leaving me, you know," I said, my voice thick with tears.

"I know."

"I hate you a little bit for doing this."

"If it's no more than usual I can handle it."

We laughed and Aiden pulled me into his arms, the familiar scent of his body making me lose the battle with my tears.

"Promise me we won't ever not be friends," I whispered, wiping at my face. "Promise me, when we're eighty we'll still annoy the fuck out of each other."

"I promise." He kissed the side of my head, and pulled away. The conviction in his voice made me believe that he meant it, even if nobody could ever make such a promise.

We'd always been fools, both of us.

"I need you to promise me something, too," Aiden said, looking more serious than I'd seen him lately. I nodded, not trusting my voice to speak. "I want you to talk to your mother." I opened my mouth to protest, but he shushed me. "Listen to me, Finney."

The command in his voice made me stop short.

"I want you to talk to her, just the two of you, without getting angry or upset at anything she says, and retaliating. I want you, for a few short moments, to put yourself in her shoes and figure out why she's acting this way. I want you to try and find a solution." I shook my head slightly, wanting to fulfil his request, but knowing nothing would come of it. Been there, done that, got the bulletproof vest.

"And if you can't find a solution," Aiden continued, pronouncing every word slowly and carefully, making me snap my eyes back to him. "I want you to get closure and walk away."

I gasped, my eyes widening. In the past, I'd shared with him how I wanted to cut off any ties with my mother, but I was too much of a coward to do it. He'd been vehemently against the idea, always finding ways to convince me that even a horrible relationship with my mother was better than a non-existent one.

Seemed like what she'd said to me in the kitchen had been the last drop for him, too.

"Okay," I managed to say. "I promise."

I wiped my face with my palm again, desperately trying to collect myself enough to see him off. I'd break down later. Right now, Aiden needed me to pull myself together. I could already see the doubt in his eyes, the silent question if he'd done the right thing by accepting this job. I wouldn't let him put his life on hold for me ever again.

"I've got something for you," I said, opening my satchel and taking the folder I'd prepared last night. "I printed this out for you so that you won't be bored on the long flight."

Taking the folder, he flicked the first page inside and, seeing a copy of my manuscript, he grinned.

"Work, work, work," he said through a smile. "It's all I'm good for, apparently."

You're good for so many other things, I thought, but kept it to myself. If I'd said it out loud the waterworks would start again and I was embarrassed enough already. So instead, I hugged my best friend tightly, one last time, and stepped away.

"You'd be coming with me if it weren't for him." He didn't raise his intonation at the end of the sentence because it wasn't a question. We stared at each other, time stopping around us, as the realisation that for the first time in ten years our lives took a different path really hit home.

I shook my head and time seemed to unfreeze, sending the travellers around us in a renewed frenzy to get to their destination on time.

"I love him," I said, holding Aiden's gaze. He nodded slowly as if finally accepting it. He was right – if it weren't for Ben I wouldn't hesitate to buy a one-way ticket and follow Aiden anywhere. But the thought of leaving Ben was even more unbearable than the thought of letting go of Aiden, so I'd never even entertained it.

"Be good." I raised my index finger at him mockingly. "Don't do anything I wouldn't do."

"That leaves quite a wide range of trouble I can get into."

We laughed, and I knew this was how I wanted the moment to end. I wanted him to be laughing and happy when he got on that plane, excited about the new life he was starting, not pining over me as he'd done for most of his life.

It was time to let Aiden go, but dammit it hurt.

"You better go," I said, pushing him lightly away. "The queue for the security is massive. I don't want you to miss your flight and be stuck here."

"Definitely not." He tried to smile but it wavered, and Aiden's expressive hazel eyes shimmered with tears.

With one last hug and a promise to call and text every day, and visit him in a few months, I turned around and left.

I couldn't watch his back as he headed for the gates. I wasn't sure if I was more scared he'd turn around and decide to stay, or that he wouldn't.

The automatic doors of the airport opened with a whoosh in front of me and a whiff of humid, August air hit my face. As he'd promised, Ben was waiting for me outside, looking anxious. I walked into his open arms, and broke, painful sobs tearing out of me until I had nothing left.

CHAPTER TWENTY THREE

September came with a wave of hot weather, even worse than the last week of August. I couldn't stand the damn heat anymore. Where was the stormy, cold weather Britain was so famous for when I most needed it? I waved a freshly printed A4 sheet in front of my face, hoping for a reprieve from the humid heat. Deciding to go work on the revisions in the garden had been a mistake, but I couldn't be bothered to move now that I'd set everything up. It was late afternoon and the sun should hide behind the trees soon, anyway.

I heard the front door open and close, thankful for the distraction. My focus was non-existent in this heat, but now I had an opportunity to blame my lack of productivity on my boyfriend. Ben stepped into the garden, looking hot as hell in his jeans, navy button-down with the sleeves rolled up, and a pair of aviator sunglasses. His hair was cut shorter than usual, despite my protests. It was still a mop of wild curls, making him look as if he was still in school instead of a college student.

I grinned at the thought.

"Hey," I said, tilting my head up to accept the kiss he leaned down to give me. "How did it go?"

Ben pulled another chair from under the table and sat with a grunt.

"The air conditioning in the student office was broken and I nearly died of heat stroke." He removed the sunglasses from his face and rubbed at his eyes. Then, as if noticing my cold bottle of water for the first time, he snatched it and gulped down half of it before I could complain.

In the morning, Ben'd been so nervous about his interview and registration at Pembroke that he'd woken up at dawn, buzzing with adrenalin and unable to sit still for a second. It'd been the first time I'd seen him like that. Usually, I was the one fretting and vibrating with energy, and Ben was the solid wall I kept crashing against.

"Okay," I drawled, claiming my water back when he placed it on the table. "Other than that, did everything go okay? Did you register?"

A slow smile appeared on Ben's face as he nodded. "I'm officially a college student, baby." He leered at me, knowing it'd make me laugh.

I left my chair in favour of straddling his lap. The flimsy garden chair creaked under our combined weight, but we both ignored it.

"A *hot* college student," I purred, draping my arms around his neck. "And all mine."

Ben hummed, sliding his hands up and down my back and pulling me down for a long, hard kiss. We broke apart, breathing heavily, grinning.

I loved seeing Ben that happy. For so long, the shadow of letting his dreams slip away had haunted him, darkening his brilliant green eyes. But once he'd found the courage to talk to his parents, his whole demeanour had changed, and he walked with a newfound spring in his step.

Ben'd asked me to be there when he'd told his parents about his decision to study Engineering. That conversation had gone as I'd predicted. Maria and Robert had not only been supportive of Ben's choice to leave the family business and study, but proud he'd been accepted at one of the most prestigious colleges in Cambridge University. Robert had even joked that hiring someone else to fill in for Ben would be much cheaper than the extortionate salary Ben'd demanded.

"What do you say we head upstairs," I said, managing a couple of words between kisses. "And get sweaty in an entirely different way?"

Before Ben could reply my damn phone rang. We groaned in unison and I was ready to reject the call when I saw it was my agent. I'd sent her the manuscript of my new book a few days ago, and she was probably just calling to confirm she'd received it. Deciding the conversation wouldn't take long, I stretched backwards towards the table, and, still sitting in Ben's lap, picked up.

"Hey, Angie."

"Finn, how are you, darling?" Angie drawled, her East London accent enveloping me like an old, soft t-shirt. Without giving me a chance to reply, she continued. "Listen, hun, I've got something to tell you, a few things actually, but I'd rather you came down to my office."

I frowned a little and Ben instinctively rubbed his hands up and down my arms.

"Is everything okay? Did you finish reading my book?" I held my breath waiting for her reply.

"Yes, darling!" She exclaimed, the tone of her voice getting livelier. "I loved it! It's one of the things I wanted to talk to you about, and maybe we can get Aiden on Skype as well. I think there are some areas that could be greatly improved by a few tweaks."

I stiffened, remembering many sessions in Angie's office with Aiden and I sitting for hours, arguing why a certain scene should stay as it was, regardless of market trends and public opinion. I really didn't want to go through that again. If I'd been unwilling to budge on my storyline when I was an eighteen-year-old baby writer, Angie could be damn sure I wasn't budging on anything right now. The difference was, before I'd been too apathetic to care if my books got published or not. This time, I cared too much for the story to remain as it was, and I was willing to fight for it.

"Um, okay..." I said, leaving her an opening to elaborate.

"Don't be like that, hun." Angie's musical laugh rang in my ears, making me wince. "I promise the news I've got is good, and I'm asking you down here so that we can celebrate together. When can you get here?"

I looked at Ben who's probably heard the conversation as we were so close, and he shrugged, then mouthed,

"Whenever."

I knew he started uni in early October, and I doubted his dad would mind giving him a couple of days off, so I arranged to meet Angie in her office Thursday morning, two days from now, and disconnected the call.

"Do you think your dad would mind if you took Thursday and Friday off?"

Ben shook his head, a smile already forming on his lips.

"Because I want to take you for a long weekend in London."

Mum, we need to talk. Meet me in Nero at Trafalgar at 10am on Friday.

I sent the text, closing my eyes with a long exhale. I couldn't be sure she'd agree, so I turned off my phone instead of staring at it and waiting for her reply, driving myself crazy. I intended to keep my promise to Aiden even if it'd taken me a month to gather the courage. I hadn't talked to my mother since my birthday, and it'd been the most peaceful month of my life. The thought that I should reach out kept nagging me from the back of my mind, but it still wasn't enough to ruin my internal peace.

It was then that I knew Aiden had been right. We either needed to find a solution and move forward with our relationship, or stay away from each other. I had no doubt I was causing her as much stress as she was causing me, and I convinced myself it would be for the best.

I heard the shower turning off in the bathroom and a moment later Ben walked in the bedroom, a towel wrapped loosely around his waist. He looked so different with his hair wet and slicked back. No less delicious, though.

Losing the towel completely, he climbed into the bed next to me.

"You alright?" He asked, brushing a loose strand of hair from my forehead.

"I finally sent my mother a text asking her to meet me."

"And?"

"I turned off my phone." By now I didn't have to explain why. He was getting a better understanding of our family dynamics every single day, mainly because I bitched about it non-stop.

"I think it's a good idea, doing it sooner rather than later," he said, kissing my neck. The fresh scent of our shower gel reached my nostrils at the same time Ben's body scent did. I groaned, running my fingers through his wet hair.

"Speaking of doing things sooner rather than later..."

With no warning, Ben grabbed me by the waist and flipped me on top of him, palming the back of my head and kissing the remaining thoughts out of my mind.

London on a fresh, autumn morning was a thing of beauty. We got off at King's Cross and took the tube to Green Park. Outside, the streets were swarmed with people, some wearing suits and clutching disposable coffee mugs for dear life; others jogging in their tight lycra work-out clothes, or walking their dogs leisurely, chatting with other dog owners. Mothers pushed buggies, teenagers lurked about in school uniforms, street vendors advertised their products loudly, delicious smells drifting through the air.

God, it was good to be back.

Taking a deep breath, I took Ben's hand in mine and led him down the street towards Angie's office. We reached her building five minutes ahead of schedule which was all Ben's doing. I'd barely been able to get up at the ungodly hour of six in the morning, going through the motions of brushing my teeth and dressing half asleep. Ben had to redo the buttons on my shirt as I'd done them crookedly, the whole time smiling affectionately at me. I hadn't appreciated it at the time, mostly glaring at him for waking me up so early when we could have easily taken a later train. But thinking about it a few hours later, fed and caffeinated, I realised how cute he'd been. Impulsively, I tugged him closer and kissed him before I opened the door of building.

The receptionist took our names and let us go up, offering to store the duffel Ben carried with our weekend getaway essentials. Angie was waiting for us when the elevator door opened, greeting us both with kisses on each cheek and a warm hug.

I hadn't seen her in person in two years, but she hadn't changed at all. She still wore her blonde hair long, tied in a slick ponytail, a thick fringe falling into her heavily made-up eyes.

After the compulsory introductions and pleasantries, we were sat in her comfortable office, Angie beaming at us from behind her desk.

"First things first," she said, placing her elbows on the desk. "Remember the small, independent company that acquired the film rights for *Lost Silence*?"

"Of course. They went under the following year and the film production was cancelled before it'd even really begun," I said with a shrug.

I didn't much care for any of my books to be adapted to film, but this company, Rubik's Cube, had sent the screenplay writer, director, *and* executive producer who'd be working on the film, to convince me. We'd had lengthy conversations and I'd been amazed how the screenplay writer's vision not only matched mine but enhanced it in a beautiful, sensual way. The director had assured me no important scenes would be changed, and the characters would be exactly as in the book, without changing their personalities, gender or sexual orientation in the hopes of reaching a wider audience.

In the end, after combing through the contract countless times to make sure everything they'd promised was in there, and there were no loopholes, I'd signed off on the rights. That same day I'd called my mother with the news, and it'd been the only time in my entire life when she hadn't said anything to make me feel inadequate. I'd even like to think she was a little proud of me.

"... and they want to revisit the contract," Angie was saying when I felt a kick to my ankle, bringing me out of my thoughts.

"Sorry, what?"

Angie sighed, her smile disappearing in favour of a glare aimed at me.

"Stop spacing out! Jesus!"

I managed to look sufficiently chastised, mumbling another apology, before she repeated what she'd said. Ben pretended to cough behind his hand, trying to hide his giggle.

"I was saying," she emphasised every word. "Mercutio has bought whatever was left of Rubik's Cube and are evaluating all their assets, including any book rights they have acquired. They want to send someone down here to renegotiate a new contract."

I spaced out again as Angie rambled about what an incredible opportunity that was and how I should at least listen to what they had to say. She went on to list the company's credentials and the ground-breaking, award winning films they'd made.

"Fine, whatever, I'll talk to them but I don't promise anything," I said moodily, already getting bored with the conversation.

"It's all I'm asking." Angie put her thick-rimmed glasses on and started rummaging through a pile of papers. "Oh, there they are." She passed me a sheet of paper titled 'notes' and I took it apprehensively. "My notes on 'Ant Hills and Butterflies'."

I skimmed through them with an impassive expression. "No," I said, tossing the sheet back on her desk.

"To which one?"

"All of them."

Angie sighed so heavily I thought she'd blow all the papers off her desk.

"I only take critique from Aiden. He's the only person I trust to make my book better without compromising on the story to make it more commercial." I leaned forward in the chair, pointing at the notes sheet. "Half of these are aimed at making the book a little less 'niche', and the other half don't make much sense. Admit it, Angie, you just want to make the book more mainstream, without taking in mind what *I* want for it."

"It's my job, Finn. What kind of an agent would I be if I didn't want to make the book as popular as it could possibly be?"

"A good agent will do that without changing half the plot."

"Fine," she grumbled, removing her glasses and massaging her temples, probably wondering how this gorgeous, calm man next to me could stand me for even a second. "Shall I get Aiden on Skype to ask what he thinks?"

I crossed my arms and nodded.

Angie started clicking buttons on her computer, turning the screen towards us when the call connected, and moved to stand between me and Ben. A moment later Aiden's smiling face appeared on the big screen.

"Hi, guys!" He said and waved. "I'm at work so we have to make this quick."

"Angie wants to ruin my book," I said with a pout before anyone else could speak.

Aiden rolled his eyes. "I doubt that, Finney."

"I just had a few suggestions that would considerably widen the target audience of the book."

She summarised her notes in a few sentences and Aiden started shaking his head even before she'd finished talking.

"No," he said.

I grinned at him.

"Why do I even bother," Angie mumbled.

"Angie, I promise you Finn and I are working hard to make this book as good as it can possibly be," Aiden said, the kindness in his hazel eyes winning Angie over, just like always. "You have nothing to worry about."

"With you two? I always have something to worry about." Her voice sounded firm but there was a hint of a smile in it, too.

We let Aiden go, with promises to talk soon.

"Real talk?" Angie began as she made her way back behind her desk and sat. "I've already let out a few feelers and several publishers are very interested in this book. Especially after rumours of a possible film adaptation of *Lost Silence* have spread. They'll buy it, on your terms, without any complaints." She crossed her arms on the desk and leaned forward. "But I think of you as a friend more than as a client, Finn. I want you to look back in a few years and be proud of your work."

I leaned forward and reached for Angie's hand. She extended it willingly, and clasped my hand in hers.

"I know, Angie." She squeezed my fingers with a soft smile. "Aiden's not giving me any free passes, you know that. He's been extremely critical of some parts of the book, and made me rewrite certain scenes until my eyes cross. Trust me, we're working on making this book awesome, but I can't work with anyone else but him."

Angie studied me for a long moment before letting go of my hand and leaning back in her chair. Working with temperamental artists was Angie's calling. She knew when to push and, even more so, when to draw back, trusting us to not let her down.

"Alright," was all she said, her mouth quirking up.

The meeting wrapped up soon after that, and when she saw us to the door, she hugged me tightly, and said,

"I'm so happy you're writing again, hun."

Looking into her warm, brown eyes I knew she meant it, and not only because she was my agent.

Ben and I spent the day walking around London, enjoying some of the last warm, sunny days before winter. I was excited to take Ben to my favourite coffee shop, the library I'd spent hours in every week. We went through my old neighbourhood where I showed him the house we used to live in and the primary school I went to, and the tiny independent bookshop I'd chosen for my first book signing. He took everything in, soaking in my past and the memories I shared with the biggest smile I'd seen on him.

After dinner, my nerves about the meeting with my mother the next day started to show. I couldn't focus on anything for longer than three seconds. I clammed up, the worst possible outcomes of the conversation playing on a loop in my head.

Ben pretended to be tired and suggested we head back to the hotel to chill. I knew he was doing it for me, and I appreciated it. Back in our room, we took a long shower together, Ben massaging my shoulders under the hot water until I started to relax. Then, he wrapped me in the fluffy duvet, snuggled beside me on the bed and we watched Netflix until my eyes started to droop.

It's nothing short of a miracle how calm I feel when he's near me, was my last thought before I drifted off to sleep.

CHAPTER TWENTY FOUR

I felt strangely calm as I waited for my mother in the coffee shop. Ben'd offered to stay with me, but I felt Mum would feel more comfortable if it was just the two of us. He was browsing the giant bookshop across the road, waiting for me. I felt a pang of guilt as I left him there, not even trying to hide his concern. I'd assured him I'd call if I needed him.

I saw my mother walking through the door, looking as poised as ever. At least on the outside. She spotted me and waved, then headed for the counter to order a drink. I drank a few sips of my hazelnut latte while I waited, for the millionth time rehearsing what I was going to say in my head.

"Hello, Finnegan," she said, placing a cup of tea on the table and taking a seat. "How are you?"

For a few minutes we talked about nothing in particular. She seemed relaxed enough, pleasant even, but I knew better. She had her armour on, just like I did, and she was waiting for me to cast the first blow.

Today, however, there would be no blows. I'd say my piece and then I'd leave. I was done with this toxic relationship, and so should she.

"Look, Mum, I need to say something, but you need to listen. Really listen," I said, wrapping my hands around the mug.

Her eyes shifted uncomfortably and she quickly glanced around to check if anybody might be eavesdropping. I couldn't care less. "You've been unhappy your entire life." She opened her mouth to protest but I lifted a hand, stopping her. "Let me say what I came here to say and then we can talk about it. Once we start going back and forth we both know where it'll go." She pursed her lips. I took a deep breath and collected my thoughts. "I can probably count on one hand the number of times I've seen you laugh. You're not happy, Mum, and haven't been for a very long time, and I think it's time you asked for help."

I paused to gauge her reaction. She kept a blank expression firmly set on her face, and in that moment I wasn't angry at her anymore. I let go of all the anger, frustration and grief she'd caused me, and instead felt sorry for her. "Renee and I will be there for you if you decide to go ahead and look for treatment for your depression. But, please, Mum, you have to do something about it before it destroys everything else in your life."

"I'm not depressed," she said indignantly, but her voice lacked conviction.

"Yes. You are."

She looked like she wanted to speak, but nothing came out of her mouth.

"And you're going to be a grandmother soon. You need to take care of yourself, if not for us, then for your grandchild."

Renee and I had discussed many times why Mum refused to acknowledge her depression when it was so obvious to everyone else. She was a highly intelligent women, she had to at least suspect she might be depressed. Renee'd said that it was a generational thing, that people her age weren't used to addressing any sort of mental health issues, and I had to agree. I could see in my mother's eyes that she knew it was true, and yet stubbornly refused to accept it.

"The relationship you and I have has always been difficult," I continued when she didn't say anything. "I know I was a horrible child and you had to deal with so much while I was growing up, and later when I moved out. I put you through a lot, I know that, and I'm sorry. But you never pulled your punches when it came to me. You were quick to retaliate – even hurt me – if that got your point across, and that's not something you do to your child, Mum. It's not how it should be."

"You hurt me, too, Finnegan, so many times I've lost count."

"I know." I licked my lips, bracing myself for what I was about to say next. "I'll go with you to therapy if you think that'll help..."

She scoffed. "I'm not going to therapy, Finnegan. Enough with this nonsense. You're trying to pin all this," she waved a hand between us, "on me. It's not going to work. You've been putting me through hell ever since you were in school, always getting into trouble, always getting mixed up with the wrong people; and then later drinking, taking drugs, and god knows what else, nearly killing yourself. How do you think I feel? I had to deal with all of that alone, your father never cared. And yet you always loved him more than me. You know why I never laughed? Because I had no reason to."

I looked for anger, frustration, even annoyance inside me, and found none. I was just sad. So damn sad that for a moment my lip trembled, but I hid it behind the coffee mug. Taking a sip of the cold latte, I pushed it aside, twined my fingers on the table and looked into my mother's angry eyes.

"Do you even realise that saying *nothing* in the past twenty five years has given you a reason to smile is not normal?"

She faltered for a second, but quickly gathered her composure.

I didn't give her a chance for another rant. "If you decide to look for help, I'll support you, one hundred percent. I'll be at every therapy session you want me to be, I'll do anything you need me to do. But if you continue to bury your head in the sand, continue to hurt me just because I hurt you first..." I licked my lips, the words catching in my throat. "I can't do it, Mum. I just can't. It's too toxic. It's making us both bitter and unhappy."

She narrowed her eyes at me. "Are you giving me an ultimatum, Finnegan?"

"Yes, Mum, I am."

I stood, unhooked my satchel from the back of the chair, and bent down to hug my mother as I passed by her.

"Goodbye, Mum. I hope, one day, you find your reason to smile."

I wiped at my face as I walked out of the coffee shop, but instead of the usual dark anger I felt after a row with my mother, I felt lighter somehow. Sad, yes; regretful that even when forced to choose between her pride – or whatever was holding her back – and her child, she'd stuck to her pride. It was her choice, and there was nothing I could do.

I found Ben in the engineering section, nose buried in a huge hardback. I hadn't called him because I needed a few minutes to compose myself, but I made an educated guess on where he could be.

"Hi," I whispered, hugging him from behind.

"Hey," he turned quickly, closing the book. He studied me, looking me over as if checking for injuries. When I smiled at him he frowned. "She agreed?"

I shook my head. "No." Ben frowned even deeper. "But I said what I had to say, and I'm done. I'm not happy about it, but I feel I finally got closure. After so many years of hurting each other."

"Maybe she'll come around?"

I kissed his nose. "Maybe. Who knows. I won't hold my breath, though. I inherited my stubbornness from her."

TEN MILE BOTTOM

Ben hugged me and we stayed like that for a little while, embracing in the deserted engineering aisle, lost in our own thoughts.

"Come on," I said, pulling away and clasping his hand. "I want you to meet someone."

I'd never been to the cemetery. When I'd run out of the church at the funeral, I never got a chance to see my dad's coffin being lowered into the ground. I'd asked Renee where he was buried and she'd given me instructions so unclear we had to walk around and peer at dozens of grave stones until we found my dad's.

There were fresh flowers in a little plastic vase and I wondered for a moment who'd left them.

"We should have brought some flowers," Ben said, shifting from foot to foot uncomfortably.

"That's okay. Dad never particularly liked flowers."

I pulled him down to sit on a small bench on one side of the grave. He seemed nervous, his foot bouncing uncharacteristically.

"When I was eight, Dad took me to my first football match," I said, taking Ben's hand in mine. "It was Chelsea versus Arsenal, and it was a big deal. The stadium was full to the brim, the roar of the crowd deafening. I remember being nervous at first, maybe even a little scared. People threw insults at one another on the stands around us and I was worried we might get caught in the middle of a fight and get hurt.

"Dad held my hand the whole time, even though I never said anything to him. I was embarrassed." I smiled, remembering it as vividly as I'd felt it back then. "I was desperate to show him I was tough, so I never said anything, but he knew. I think, in his own way, he wanted to show me that it was okay if sometimes we weren't as tough as we thought we should be."

Ben swung an arm around my shoulders and pulled me closer to kiss my temple. We stayed like this for a while, and I told him some other stories about my dad. I didn't particularly believe in the afterlife, or God, or the eternal soul. But sitting here with Ben, talking about my dad, remembering him at his best, made me feel closer to him than I'd ever been when he was alive.

"My biggest regret is not having a proper relationship with him." I glanced at the grave stone, a silent apology to him echoing in my head. "I can blame my mother for it all I want, but the truth is, I should have fought harder for it."

"You were just a kid, Finn. It's hard to fight your parents, especially a strong-willed one like your mother, when you're just a kid."

"I don't know. Maybe you're right." I sighed heavily, letting all the sadness, regret, and grief leak out of me. "I'm just...sorry. I can't turn back time and change anything, but what I can do is never let that soul-consuming apathy ever claim me again." I turned to Ben, taking his head between my palms and looking into his eyes. "I love you, Ben. And I'm so grateful to whatever made me point to Ten Mile Bottom on a map, and I met you."

Ben smiled, leaning in to place a chaste kiss on my lips.

"Maybe it was your dad's spirit."

"Maybe it was."

CHAPTER TWENTY FIVE

There was something about sex in a hotel that made the experience that much hotter.

I ran my hands over Ben's body as he moved above me, riding me into oblivion. I'd forbidden him from touching his cock, and it bobbed up and down, hard and leaking, the vein on the underside bulging with the need to come. Ben bounced in slow, measured moves, working his prostate on my cock, teasing me, knowing I needed more, too. I bit my lip, grabbing his hands and holding them behind his back. He seemed to like that even more. The smirk he gave me as he watched me under hooded lids told me he was enjoying the endless teasing just as much as I was.

Not letting go of his hands, I sat up, making him gasp as my cock buried even deeper inside him. Getting control of the situation, I urged Ben backwards, pumping my hips into him while he fucked down on me.

It was glorious. My whole body tingled like a live wire, ready to burst into tiny pieces of pleasure at any moment. If Ben's increasingly loud moans and jerky movements were anything to go by, he was close too.

"Fuck, Finn," he rasped, the veins on his arms bulging as he supported himself on the mattress. "I'm going to come. Just like that, baby."

I was nailing his sweet spot with every thrust, but I was so close myself I didn't know if I'd be able to make him come like this.

"Touch yourself," I said with effort.

"No." Ben threw his head back, his hips losing their rhythm, his sweat slick skin slapping against mine. He came with a hoarse shout, and I pumped his dick a few times, making sure he'd gotten everything out of his orgasm.

"My turn," I said, grabbing him by the waist and placing him flat on his back, my thighs trembling as I thrust hard inside him a couple of times before I was coming.

I collapsed on top of him, panting, my lips dry as I licked them before we kissed. He wrapped his arms loosely around me, kissing me back leisurely, murmuring words of appreciation.

Later, as we lay in bed, freshly showered and pleasantly drowsy, I gathered the courage to say something that'd been on my mind ever since he got registered at the university.

"So, um..." I began, feeling Ben shift slightly underneath me. I didn't raise my head from his chest as I spoke. "I was thinking that you have no reason to travel back and forth to Ten Mile Bottom now that you'll be studying back in Cambridge and won't be working for your dad anymore." Ben hummed, tracing circles on my shoulder as he waited to see where I was going with this. "So that means I won't see you as often, and that's not acceptable." I felt him grin, but he still said nothing. Bastard. He was going to make me do all the work. "So how about you help me look for a flat in Cambridge so that we can see each other more often?"

I bit my lip and held my breath while he took his damn time to reply.

"Hm, no, I don't think that works for me," he said.

I lifted my head off his chest sharply, frowning at him.

"Why not?"

"Because I was going to suggest we look for a flat in Cambridge for both of us."

It took me a moment to realise what he was saying. He couldn't hold his serious face any longer, so he smiled widely at me and lifted his head to kiss the corner of my mouth.

"Let's move in together."

"Are you sure?"

Ben held my gaze, the tenderness in his eyes leaving little room for doubt. "Absolutely."

EPILOGUE

9 months later

My fingers flew over the keyboard as I was trying to finish this chapter before Ben got home. We always had dinner together, no matter what, but if I left a paragraph or two for later it'd bug me the whole time we ate. My phone buzzed on the coffee table but I ignored it. Just a few more sentences and I'd hit my word goal for the day, and wrap up the chapter.

When it was done, I saved the document and closed the laptop, standing up to stretch my legs. For the past few months I'd spend my time writing while Ben was in school, and it was paying off. Not only was I getting more prolific, I actually felt better. I had considerably less free time, but I was doing something with my life and it made me happy.

My phone buzzed again, demanding my attention. I swiped it off the table and unlocked the screen

She's so cute when she sleeps. I almost forget the sound of her screams.

I chuckled at my sister's text, and the photo she'd attached of baby Sam. She really was the cutest thing ever, with chubby cheeks and huge blue eyes, and the most charming smile. But, man, she could scream. Ben and I had offered to babysit last weekend, to give Renee and Luis a chance to get out for a little while without a three-month-old attached to them. I'd regretted it the moment they left. Unsurprisingly, Ben had been amazing with her, and she'd taken a liking to him straight away, sleeping happily in his arms while she screamed the moment I came within two feet of her.

Closing the messaging app, I pulled up my email and found several unanswered emails from Angie. She wanted to set up another meeting next week with the film people from Marcutio in the first email, wanted me to reconsider a promotional tour for *Ant Hills and Butterflies* which was coming out in two weeks in the second, and wanted me to reply to my fucking emails in the most recent.

I typed a quick response, confirming the time and date for the film meeting, but declining, for what seemed like the eleven millionth time, the stupid promotional tour. I wasn't cut out for that shit, I reminded her, and would probably put people off the book if they let me loose on a promotional tour. Mostly, I couldn't be bothered, and we both knew it, so I really hoped she'd stop pestering me. I finished the email with several kiss emojis to annoy her, and closed the app.

Just as I was heading for the kitchen to start making dinner, I got another message. With an exasperated sigh I grabbed my phone and found a text from Rose.

Have you found me a flat in Cambridge yet?

I rolled my eyes.

Have you received your exam results yet?

We both knew she hadn't – they were to come out in August – but she was so confident she'd done well that she was already looking for a flat. She refused to live in the dorm, and she was planning on working part time on top of her scholarship – or student loan in case she didn't get one – so she thought she could afford it. Plus, she wanted to take Eren with her, and pets weren't allowed in the student dorm. I was impressed with her ambition and determination. Of course, I'd never tell her that.

I know I did awesome, Cambridge will be begging me to go there.

With all that confidence one would think you'd be able to find your own damn flat.

She sent me the middle finger emojis and I didn't bother justifying that with a reply.

"Now, can I go cook dinner for my boyfriend?" I said to the phone, tossing it onto the kitchen table. It buzzed a few more times as I cooked, but I ignored it. Rose'd made me reactivate all my social media accounts last month in preparation for the release of my new book, and the damn notifications never stopped. I appreciated that people still remembered who I was after all this time, considering the non-existent attention span of the current generation, but I had to figure out how to stop all that buzzing before I threw my phone out the window.

I made pasta, because it was easy and we didn't have the ingredients for anything else. We needed to go grocery shopping very soon, but with Ben's gruelling schedule, we could barely find the time. I didn't want to waste a second of my weekends with him to go to the supermarket, hence the nearly empty fridge.

The front door opened and closed in quick succession and a few seconds later Ben appeared at the kitchen doorway.

"Mmm, smells amazing," he said, coming to kiss me. "Thank you."

He came home starving every day, not always able to grab lunch if he had to study in the library. My boyfriend was an ambitious overachiever if I ever saw one. His professors were impressed with him, and giving him additional tasks for extra credits, but unfortunately that usually stole his lunch break.

"I have news!" He announced, grabbing me by the hand and leading me to the sofa. I looked back longingly at the plates piled with pasta on the table, but followed him without complaint. "Remember that summer apprenticeship I applied for in January?"

"How can I not? I *made* you do it," I said pointedly.

"I got it." He beamed like the fucking sun, but it took me a while to get what he was actually saying.

"Wait, what? Really?" He nodded enthusiastically. "But you said Professor Hale told you they rarely picked anyone in their first year."

Ben shrugged. "I know, that's what he told me, but Honda wants me. Who am I to object?"

A slow smile tugged at my lips and I leaned into him, hugging him tight.

"Congratulations, baby," I pulled back. "So, what does that mean exactly?"

"It means we're going to Tokyo for two months!"

Out of all the apprenticeships offered, we'd picked the one in Tokyo because Ben's heart was set on working for Honda, whose headquarters was in Tokyo, and I was desperate to see Aiden. But we never actually believed it would happen, especially when Ben'd heard under the grapevine that he was the only first year who'd had the confidence to apply.

"I mean..." He hesitated for a moment, some of the excitement draining out of him. "If that's okay with your mum. It's not going to disturb your sessions, right?"

Four months after our talk, and a day after Sam was born, my mother had showed up at my door and broken down in tears. We'd welcomed her in, fed her a good meal, and put her to bed in our bedroom while we shared the sofa. In the morning, over a cup of coffee, she'd said she wanted to get better and had booked an appointment with a therapist. She'd asked me to go with her once a week at first, and then a couple of times a month. Renee also had her own session with Mum, but they were less regular because of the baby.

I wasn't expecting miracles. Mum had a long, hard road ahead of her, but as I'd promised, I was there for her. Our relationship had gotten better, but we still had our moments when we needed to be away from each other or we'd scratch each other's eyes out. The main difference was that we talked now. When something was bothering her, she'd come and tell me instead of lashing out, and I did the same.

"I'm sure she wouldn't mind if we skip a few sessions," I said. "Now, can we go eat before I faint?"

Ben laughed and pulled me up, wrapping an arm around my waist as we walked back to the kitchen. Swirling spaghetti around my fork, my thoughts drifted to this time last year when I was a lonely recovering addict, desperately trying to escape not only London's toxic influence, but hiding away from my own life. As it'd turned out, it wasn't London that was toxic, it was the demons inside me. I still fought those demons every single day, and some days it was harder than others. But Ben's unwavering support, even when I felt moody and unreasonably bitter, helped me in a way I could've never imagined.

We were the exact opposites of each other, but I knew we were the yin and yang of the same soul. Not many people could say they'd found their soulmate, or even believed such things existed, and this time last year I was one of them.

What a difference a year makes.

THE END

TEN MILE BOTTOM

AUTHOR'S NOTE

Thank you for reading this book!

As I said in the short note in the beginning of the book, this story is very personal to me. Finn is closer to me than any of my other characters, and has to deal with a lot of stuff I've dealt with, and still have to deal with. I've always been a bit wary of writing from personal experience, but Finn's character insisted I gave him the opportunity to tell his story. And, as we've seen, he can be a dick if you ignore him.

But it wasn't until my beloved BMW left me stranded close to a little town called Six Mile Bottom, its power steering giving out, that Ten Mile Bottom was born. I actually started writing notes on the story in the tow truck. And yes, the car was working perfectly when we unloaded it, just like Finn's, but my mechanic wasn't as sexy as Ben.

Finn's relationship with his mother was the hardest thing I've ever had to write, mainly because it's so close to my own reality. Some of the conversations they have are word for word what my mother and I have said to each other, and writing that down was painful. I'm glad Finn got a chance to work on that relationship, and mend it over time.

As for dear, sweet Ben... I adore that guy, and I'm lucky to have a real Ben in my life, always supporting me even when I don't feel like I'm worth supporting.

A lot of my early readers have asked if Aiden is getting his own book, so I feel I should mention this here: YES! Aiden is getting his own book later this year, set in Tokyo, and there will be a cameo from Finn and Ben, too. I'm actually going to Japan in a couple of weeks, so I'm super excited to do the research for the book there.

Thank you again for reading, and I hope you enjoyed this book. Leaving a review on Amazon, Goodreads and anywhere else you may fancy will be super helpful and much appreciated. X

CONTACTS

Blog: www.teodorakostova.blogspot.com
Twitter: https://twitter.com/Teodora_Kostova
Facebook: https://www.facebook.com/teodorakostovaauthor
Facebook group: https://www.facebook.com/groups/245720345600711/
Instagram: www.instagram.com/teodorika1
Newsletter: https://goo.gl/gwytxF

ALSO BY TEODORA KOSTOVA

West End series

Dance

Mask

Dreaming of Snow

Piece by Piece

Snowed In

Cookies

A Sip of Rio

Kiss and Ride

Heartbeat series

In a Heartbeat

Then, Now, Forever

Printed in Great Britain
by Amazon